TEXAS COWBOY SHERIFF

BARB HAN

TorJake Publishing

To my family for unwavering love and support. I can't imagine doing life with anyone else.

CHAPTER ONE

"Good morning, Mrs. Brubaker."

As she spoke, Laurel Roberts immediately crossed the room to the window. She whisked open the floor-length curtains to bathe the room in sunlight. The almost pitch-black room of one of her favorite residents might be good for sleeping, but it was time to rise and shine. Laurel had an unexplained soft spot for the silver-haired occupant in room number seven at Resting Acres, despite Hattie Brubaker's onery side. In fact, Laurel probably liked the centenarian *because* of it.

As Laurel glanced out at the yard, a habit she'd picked up nine months ago after fleeing Chicago, she could have sworn a male figure darted behind a tree trunk. Panic squeezed her chest as she stared out the window, studying the tree, watching for any sign she could trust her eyes, and that her imagination hadn't just gone wild.

Heart racing, gaze focused, she gasped when a gust of wind knocked a few leaves loose. Hand over her mouth, she suppressed a scream. It was fine. This wasn't Chicago. She'd gone to great lengths to ensure there was no trail. He couldn't possibly have found her.

"Are you an angel?" Hattie asked in dramatic fashion after clearing her throat. Laurel gave the tree a last once-over before turning in time to see Hattie make a show of rubbing her eyes like she couldn't believe what she was seeing.

"Nope. Just me. Laurel," she responded, adding quietly, "no one special."

"Come closer, heavenly child. My eyesight isn't what it used to be," the elder resident continued, seemingly unfazed by reality. The woman played the age card better than a World Championship Poker player played Texas Hold 'em.

"I'm right here," Laurel said with a forced smile. The sun was rising on what would be another warm day in early fall. The temperatures in her former hometown had already dipped below freezing. Not here. Texas was just as she remembered, warm and sunny. She would take flip-flops over snow boots this time of year, any day of the week. A change of seasons wasn't due for another week or so in Gunner, Texas, and the short-lived leaf show had yet to begin.

"It's bright out there," Mrs. Brubaker said, pushing up to sitting position.

"Another one for the books," Laurel confirmed with a smile. "Can I make you a cup of coffee before I head out?"

Mrs. Brubaker patted the bed. "How much longer until your shift is over?"

Laurel checked her watch. "Technically, I'm done,

but there's no way I would walk out of here without saying good morning," she said.

"Sit with an old lady for a few minutes before you go?" Mrs. Brubaker was turning on the puppy dog eyes, making it impossible to say no.

"Of course," Laurel relented, feeling every minute of her ten-hour shift in her aching feet. Mentally, she'd clocked out half an hour ago. But how could she refuse?

"Are you sure you don't want coffee? I don't mind running out for some. The staff lounge is practically right outside your door," Laurel said.

"Well, if it's no trouble," Mrs. Brubaker conceded with a twinkle in her eyes. She loved breaking the rules and this was a huge no-no. Residents had their own kitchenettes, bathroom, and living/bedroom combination. They were supposed to stock their own minifridges and cabinets.

"I'll be back faster than you can put your teeth in," Laurel teased.

"Challenge accepted." The older woman immediately reached for the glass on the nightstand where those pearly whites were soaking.

Laurel continued playing along, hurrying out of the room. It was technically shift change, so the other attendants would be making rounds. As long as the head nurse, a.k.a. Nurse Ratched, didn't catch Laurel, they would be fine. That reminded her. She probably should have grabbed a cup from Mrs. Brubaker's room. Laurel bit back a curse.

She rushed into the lounge, praying Ratched wouldn't be waiting in the hallway. The woman had a sixth sense about these kinds of incidents. She seemed to know exactly when to swoop in and bust attendants for the slightest infraction, and the term 'playful' meant nothing. She excelled at medical care for the residents though, so at least she had that working for her.

This time, Laurel made it back to the room with the contraband coffee without bumping into a soul. This day was starting to look up, if she ignored the creepy-crawly feeling that still lingered after that moment at the window. After a quick visit with Mrs. Brubaker, Laurel would head home to the lake where her kayak would be waiting. Getting out on the water in early November wasn't something she could do without freezing her backside off back home. This was the reason she'd chosen Texas as a place to hide. Plus, she'd never spoken about her time here with anyone up north. The Lone Star State might not be the last place on earth anyone would search for her, but it was close.

"Here you go," she said to a waiting Mrs. Brubaker. "I managed to sneak it out."

The toothy smile staring at her from the bed made Laurel laugh as she handed over the drink.

"Don't get yourself in trouble over me," Mrs. Brubaker said, but the hint of mischief in her eyes said she loved these little games and that she also knew she'd won. This incredible woman had been the first from Texas to swim the English Channel; she'd survived losing two of her three children to Vietnam, and a husband to 'the big C word' as she'd put it; plus, she'd written a physics paper in the nineties that was still being used for core teaching at the University of Texas at Austin. She'd been a spitfire, a real force to be reckoned with, who now spent most of her days sitting at the window reading or looking at pictures of days gone by. Her daughter and granddaughter visited Sundays. They seemed to love her. Laurel had even overheard Ruthie, the daughter, beg her mother to come live with them. Mrs. Brubaker laughed off the request, saying she'd be in the way.

Laurel wanted to ask why, but gathered the subject was touchy.

"Tell me about Chicago this time of year," Mrs. Brubaker said, patting a spot next to her.

"Well, it's cold for one thing," Laurel stated with a visible tremor, before perching on the side of the bed. She'd answered the older woman's question honestly about where she'd come from, praying it wasn't a mistake. The words had slipped out a little too easily, and Laurel had had to remind herself not to be so chatty with people. Impossible with present company, she thought. Lying was hard. Laurel had never developed a gift for deception. "But that's just a preamble for what's to come when the real cold strikes."

"I bet the snow is beautiful, though." There was a wistful quality to Mrs. Brubaker's eyes as she sipped the warm coffee, no doubt wishing she could be on another adventure instead of this bed.

"You won't get any argument from me there," Laurel said. "There is something magical about those tiny white flakes drifting down from the heavens."

Mrs. Brubaker's smile widened at the image.

"My husband couldn't take the cold," she said on a sigh. "Of course, I've always believed anything in the seventies is sweater and coat weather." She laughed and some of the spark returned to her eyes.

A knock at the door interrupted their easy conversation.

"How are you doing today, Ms. B?" Tad Durant asked, stepping inside the room before being given permission to enter. The intern always seemed to pop in whatever room Laurel was in at the end of her ten-hour shift. She bit back a yawn and forced a smile. Technically, Tad had seniority over her. Upsetting him or making him an enemy wouldn't be in her best interest, but she still wished he'd give her some space.

"I'm finer than a frog hair split four ways," Mrs. Brubaker announced proudly as she threw the covers off and swung her feet off the bed. Her flannel nightgown fell well past her knees and Laurel noticed how the older woman had slipped the coffee onto the dresser without Tad batting an eye.

"Good to hear," Tad said. He'd insisted Laurel call him by his first name. She thought it sounded a little too chummy.

"Besides, Laurel is right here if I need anything," the older woman stated.

Tad was just shy of six feet tall with a runner's build. He had dark hair, cobalt blue eyes that seemed to work wonders on the other attendants. His charms didn't have the same effect on Laurel, and she feared it had caused him to double down on his efforts to convince her.

"Speaking of which," he started, turning toward Laurel. "How about we grab a cup of coffee when your shift is over?"

He'd barely delivered his line before firing off a wink. Seriously? All she could think was how badly she wanted to take a shower to scrub off the used car salesman yuck after this conversation with him. Not only was Tad not her typical type, but he gave her the creeps. And, sure, her radar was up despite moving to a town where no one knew her name or background. Laurel had gone to great lengths to ensure no one found her, especially not...

She shivered.

"No, thanks," she said, refocusing on Tad's question. "I'm expected at home."

It wasn't a complete lie. More like stretching the truth to let him down easy. This was the fourth day in a row he'd asked, and this was the fourth time she'd turned him down. Thankfully, she was off the next three days. Maybe by then he would move on to another attendant.

And her kayak was expecting her. Sort of. As much as an inanimate object could wait for someone.

It might have been nine months since she'd left the small suburb on the outskirts of Chicago, but her ordeal had started almost two years prior. The death. The accusation. The harassment. No one wanted to believe she was innocent, or that she'd acted in self-defense. Least of all her ex's family—a family who had money, power, and ties. Soon after the investigation closed and she was deemed a victim rather than a suspect, local cops started harassing her. One in particular made her skin crawl thinking about him and the way he'd backed her up against the wall in her kitchen and threatened to do things to her she'd since blocked from her mind. Ricky Harris. Thinking about him now caused an involuntary shiver to rock her body.

Breathe.

Laurel was confident in the place she'd chosen to hide. Originally from the outskirts of Chicago, she'd headed south the minute she feared her and the lives of the people she loved were in danger after being harassed for a crime she didn't commit.

The small ranching community of Gunner had been a safe haven for the past three months. There was a dozen or so founding ranching families still in the cattle business and then, of course, there was the Quinn family. They were beyond rich. She'd heard good things about their character and had heard there'd been some kind of reckoning with the patriarch. She'd also noticed all attention was on them when one or more of them was in the room. Flying under the radar meant staying as far away from the noteworthy and wealthy Quinn family as much as possible.

Gunner had a small downtown area, complete with an idyllic Main Street. Quaint shops with local flair and eateries lined the streets leading to the town hall. A feed store was at the edge of town; its parking lot was almost always full. Gunner and the surrounding area had many lakes, and that was a very large part of the reason Laurel had chosen this place for her next stop. Harmony Lake had lived up to the promise of its name. Here, time seemed to slow down and Laurel felt like she could breathe again after holding her breath for what felt like an eternity.

The job at Restful Acres had offered a lifeline. The opening had provided the other thing Laurel had needed most, an opportunity to work while most people slept. Then there was Mrs. Brubaker. She had the same hopeful powder blue eyes of Laurel's grandmother.

The incident at Mrs. Brubaker's window still had Laurel's nerves on edge. Just when she was finally starting to relax and believe she might not have to look over her shoulder for the rest of her life, something like that always happened and threw her off-kilter all over again.

Refocusing on the conversation going on between Tad and Mrs. Brubaker, Laurel saw an opportunity to duck out of the room when Tad moved closer to the bed.

She made a show of glancing at her watch as they met at the midpoint of the room. He sidestepped in time to block her view of the door, causing all of her internal alarm bells to sound.

"Look at the time," she said with a shrug, doing her level best to calm her racing pulse and quiet her fight, freeze, or flight instinct.

This time, she wouldn't allow anyone else to have control over her. She squared her shoulders and forced herself to look Tad dead in the eyes.

"Excuse me," she said with a calm she didn't feel. "And if you don't step out of the way soon, I'll move you myself."

Tad's gaze widened in what looked like surprise before he took a dramatic step to the side and swept his hand, as though giving her permission to exit.

It took pretty much all of Laurel's self-control not to comment. Instead, she took a slow breath as she walked past and muttered, *jerk,* just loud enough for him to hear, but studiously ignored his reaction.

"Behave yourself while I'm gone, Mrs. Brubaker," Laurel said with a breezy confidence she didn't own.

"Well, that doesn't sound like any fun," the older woman quipped.

"Then, at least don't get caught," Laurel said. She paused long enough at the door to glance at the bed where Mrs. Brubaker sat. The woman winked and gave a thumbs-up as Tad moved to the foot of the bed. Laurel realized instantly her friend had probably heard the remark. The encouragement gave Laurel another boost of confidence as she headed out the door and toward home.

———

Laurel admired the way the light reflected off the waves of the lake. The water shimmered underneath the morning sunshine. There was no place that felt as much like home as this cabin despite its small size. The whole place was basically two rooms with a bathroom off to one side, and a laundry nook that was tucked away in a closet hallway. The kitchenette wasn't exactly big family Thanksgiving material, but the space fit her perfectly. She could hear noises from any part of the cabin, so no one would be able to quietly break in the living room while she was sleeping in the bedroom. She'd figured out the first evening that she could leave the door open during a shower and still hear noises in the next room, like if glass broke. She'd asked her landlord to install an alarm, lost the argument. He had agreed to install a deadbolt with a signed year-long lease.

It was a shame that she might have to move again.

And it was a crying shame that her time here in Gunner might be coming to an end. Laurel reminded herself not to get too ahead of the game. It was only a possible sighting, she thought as she turned the car engine off after pulling up next to the cabin, unable to shake the neck-hairs-standing-on-end feeling that someone might be watching her. She paused long enough to glance around and saw nothing but inlet, trees, and the cabin directly across the water from hers. When she really thought about it, anyone could be hiding behind one of those trees.

The inlet opened up at the end of her lane into a massive lake that boaters frequented. She'd used the kayak a couple of times that came with the rental and had made it habit after a ten-hour workday, since it helped her unwind. There was a time when she would have had a glass of wine instead. Not any longer. She needed a clear mind at all times.

Laurel needed to get inside, throw her stuff down, and change clothes. She'd been looking forward to her usual after work kayak ride for the entire ride home. There was no better way to relax after a ten-hour shift than to get out onto the water. But then, she'd always been a water baby. In Chicago, that had meant hot baths. Here, she could get outside much of the year based on the weather patterns.

As she rounded the front of her vehicle, a noise startled her. Her hand immediately came up to her chest as the trash can tipped over, clanking against the brick wall before bouncing off and then landing against the hard soil.

Laurel screamed before her brain could process the

fact that it was a cat slinking out, shaking each paw one at a time.

"Henry, I told you not to scare me like that," Laurel fussed at the feral cat that seemed completely non-plussed by her presence. Henry had been her only visitor in the three months since she'd moved into Casa Amarillo, named for its bright yellow decorations.

Taking a moment to will her stress levels down, she breathed in a couple of deep breaths. Then, she started to clean up the mess the little tabby had made.

"What were you after?" she asked, clutching at her heart.

Shake it off, she said to herself. She was seeing shadows where there were none and freaking out over a cat in the trash can. This wasn't the first time Henry had gone foraging for food. It wouldn't be the last. The trash can had banged against the wall in the past while she'd been inside the cabin and it had scared her half to death then too. Every noise still caused her to jump, even if she no longer shrank. Now, when adrenaline surged, she bucked up for a fight.

This also signaled she had probably stayed in the same place for too long and that was truly regrettable.

On a sigh, she picked up the can and scooped up the debris using a flattened cereal box. More critters would get into it, as well as creepy-crawlies, if she didn't get this cleaned up as soon as possible.

"I hope you got something good to eat out of this, sir," she said to Henry. He seemed to have survived the initial shock of the experience as he was sitting on his hindquarters, casually licking his paws. Laurel shook her head. If she was smart, she would stop feeding him. But he needed her, and she had no plans to stop even if the little guy did cause trouble.

The mess was tidied up in a matter of minutes and yet her nerves were probably going to be fried for the rest of the day. All she could think of was getting the kayak on the water and paddling through her tension.

Inside, the cabin had a sofa and two chairs circled around a small fireplace. Having a fireplace at all caused her to scratch her head. It seemed wholly unnecessary in Texas, but, hey, she intended to use it if the temperature dipped below freezing. Cold temperatures happened in Texas. They just didn't stick around. A small round table with a flap down was pushed up against the back of the couch. Three wooden chairs were tucked underneath. Yellow accents brightened up the place and there were the softest, checkered-patterned curtains hanging on the window above the sink.

The duvet on the bed was eggshell white, and there was a bright yellow afghan folded across the bottom. It reminded her of something her beloved grandmother would have made. To Laurel, the owner had missed the mark on the name of the place. He should have named it Casa del Sol, home of the sun.

In a hurry to change into her swimsuit and cover so she could get out onto the lake before the sun scorched, it barely registered when Laurel had grabbed the handle that she realized she'd forgotten to lock the door. Shock seized her. She was getting too comfortable here. Panic gripped her, causing her chest to squeeze and her pulse to skyrocket.

This seemed like a good time to remind herself to

breathe. She was already on high alert after the 'incident' with the tree, if she could call it that, and then moments ago with Henry. Then there was Tad, who'd made leaving work stressful. Next shift, she would figure out a way to say hello to Mrs. Brubaker without crossing over with him. She was too easy to figure out. She'd set a pattern, which was exactly against the advice of the private security consultant who'd taken pity on her and given her advice before leaving Chicago. The two of them had gone over her options over an hour lunch, which was all she could afford without knowing where she would be going or how long she would be out of work.

Laurel changed as fast as humanly possible, still trying to shake the 'dark cloud over her head' feeling. Since coming to Gunner, she'd come so close to shedding it like a coat that had grown too small. In the kitchen, she made a quick protein shake and polished it off as quickly as possible. There was something about the routine of coming home, changing, and then having a protein shake before heading out for a morning row after work that was comforting. Anticipation mounted as she thought about the pale blue sky with white puffy clouds that waited outside the door. The freedom of being on the lake, gliding across the water. The stillness of the lake when there were little to no other people or boats around. Here, she'd been flying under the radar. She'd even managed to avoid the county's sheriff, Griffin Quinn. After being stalked and threatened by a dirty cop, she had no use for either.

Those thoughts were almost enough to start easing the tension that had built up between her shoulder blades and seemed to take up permanent residence since this whole ordeal began. But she didn't want to think about it while the lake called to her. Setting those thoughts aside, she moved outside.

Laurel stretched out her arms as she stepped onto the creaky wooden porch of the rental. She closed and locked the door behind her, double-checking the lock before sliding the key inside the small slit in the waistband of her swim shorts. She pulled her bright yellow kayak behind her as she moved toward the water's edge.

On the shoreline, she didn't even make it to the water when a snake hissed at her. Its head poked out of the grass lining the water, and it came at her. For a split second, Laurel froze. Then, she inched backward a step. She'd been warned about this type of snake from her landlord, but hadn't seen one in the three months since she'd moved in. There'd been spiders and other creepy crawlers, but nothing like this.

It hissed again.

A scream escaped before she could suppress it. A jolt of adrenaline coursed through her veins and she fought against the urge to freeze.

All she could think to do was let out another scream that seemed to carry across the lake and, quite probably, could be heard all the way in Seattle. There had to be some way to scare the snake, that only hissed even more.

Laurel bent down and grabbed an oar while keeping one eye on the snake. All she could think to do in the moment was slap the oar against the hard soil. She must have gotten a whole lot stronger in the past nine months because the oar cracked in half. Her attempt to scare the snake backfired as it launched toward her.

She jumped up and down, smacking what was left of the oar against the earth while screaming bloody murder. Out of the corner of her eye, she caught sight of a fishing boat speeding toward her, no doubt, to the rescue.

The man inside was unmistakable. Sheriff Griffin Quinn.

CHAPTER TWO

Laurel Roberts knew how to stay out of sight. In the three months she'd lived in Griffin Quinn's county, Griffin had seen her barely a handful of times. Most of those were of her backside as she climbed into the old pickup truck she'd bought for a song from old man McWaters. Not that Griff was stalking her. He had happened to be close enough to catch a glimpse of the transaction as it went down. Mr. McWaters had been pleased as punch he'd been able to help someone out with a vehicle sitting in his drive, collecting dust as he'd said. He'd spilled the details inside the feed store while standing in line behind Griff after the sale.

Griff had been tempted half a dozen times to check her in the system to see if he could find information about the town's newest resident. But she'd gone to great lengths to have her privacy, and since she hadn't broken the law, he'd had no reason to intrude. Until now.

Watching as she batted at the ground with a broken oar while jumping up and down, screaming, he'd changed directions with his fishing boat and made a beeline for her instead. Despite being long overdue for real time off, he'd only managed an occasional late morning fishing trip and this was one of his favorite lakes.

Griff docked and tied off his boat so it wouldn't drift away while he handled the situation. Times like these, he wished he kept a snake snatcher tool. At least, that was what he called the long metal stick with a gripper at the end.

"Water moccasin," Ms. Roberts said, still hopping up and down while batting a broken oar at the ground.

"They can be spiteful creatures," he said as he neared, his gaze constantly skimming the ground. The weeds had grown up near the edge of the water and there were several large rocks a snake might enjoy sunbathing on. In most cases, snakes did their best to stay away from humans. "Had a cousin who had to shoot one of these once, because it wouldn't stop attacking his boat."

These snakes were venomous. She was right about the type too, he realized as he got a good look. They had bodies that were thick and heavy for their length, with short, thick tails just like this one.

"I was minding my own business when he came at me from seemingly out of nowhere," Ms. Roberts said with wide eyes and labored breath. The blonde-haired, blue-eyed beauty was taller than he'd realized. At this distance he could also see a dotting of freckles on otherwise sun-kissed skin. Normally, freckles wouldn't be considered sexy and yet on her, they worked. And she didn't take her gaze off the gaping reptile. Its tail vibrated faster than a rattle in a child's hand. The troublesome part was the creature was making no attempt to escape.

"It's possible you scared him. Let's take a step back," Griff stated in a calm voice.

"What if he strikes?" Ms. Roberts asked, reaching out to grab Griff's arm with her free hand. The jolt of electricity felt like the equivalent of a lightning strike. He ignored the impact she had on him.

"I'm betting we'll be fine if we go slow," he reassured. Most folks didn't know cottonmouths, a.k.a. water moccasins, were considered more toxic than copperheads. This one was agitated and in defensive mode, which wasn't a good combination. If Griff had to guess, he'd say she caught this one off guard.

"Okay. I'll trust you know what you're doing." She sucked in a breath like she was steading herself to take a punch, before moving slowly backwards.

Once they were safely out of striking range, Griff pulled his cell from his pocket and made the call to Hank at the Department of Wildlife. A minute later, Hank promised to be on his way.

"I have a guy coming to handle this, since my vehicle isn't parked anywhere around here," Griff said. "You can hang onto the oar, but I doubt the snake will strike at this distance. Since it is holding its ground, I doubt it's going anywhere either."

"How long before your person arrives?" Ms. Roberts

asked. Griff tried not to be offended at the fact she seemed uneasy at the thought of spending a minute longer with him than was absolutely necessary.

"Hank said he was twenty to thirty minutes out, depending on traffic," Griff informed. "You can go on inside, if you don't want to stand out here with me and wait."

"Okay," she said before dropping the oar. The woman couldn't seem to get away from him fast enough.

Griff stood there, waiting. Five minutes ticked by. Then, ten. At the twenty-minute mark, he realized this was probably as good a time as any to check his work messages. Sherry Arnold was his secretary and right hand. The sixty-eight-year-old had been threatening to retire for the past six years. She wasn't the type though; Sherry got bored taking vacation days.

Before he could make the call, the door opened in the cabin behind him. Griff kept his eye on the snake.

"Sorry about my manners," Ms. Roberts said, as he heard her walk up behind him. "Would you like something to drink? Iced tea? Water?"

"Water, if it's not too much trouble," he said, wondering about the mystery woman even more, now that he'd had an interaction with her.

"I've got a bottle right here," she said, coming up beside him.

He thanked her and then took the offering. "I'm Griff, by the way," he said, figuring he didn't need to formally introduce himself as sheriff.

"I know who..." She paused, seeming to think better of continuing.

Griff took note of the odd behavior. There were plenty of reasons folks moved to a small town like Gunner out of the blue. Topping the list was a wish for privacy. Many locals stayed here for the wide-open skies and the endless acreage. People moved here for the peace and quiet. This was the place folks came to leave city life behind, embrace nature, and live a quieter life. Of those folks, quite a few didn't want to be pestered by strangers or checked up on by law enforcement. It was the number one reason they bought acreage, to put distance between themselves and everyone else. Griff didn't take those wishes lightly and never imposed on folks without an invitation.

And yet, there was something troubling in Ms. Roberts' eyes that caused him to want to know more about her. Where did she come from? Was she escaping from someone or something, or just seeking out a peaceful place where she would be left alone? A protective instinct in him stirred, and he shifted uncomfortably.

City folks moved here to escape traffic and constant drains on their time. They usually moved back within a few months, saying it was too boring or there wasn't enough excitement. This life wasn't for everyone. Some didn't realize how much they needed the buzz of filled roadways and constant noise until they met silence.

"I'm Laurel," she finally said, as Griff took a long pull off the water bottle.

"Nice to officially meet you, Laurel," he said.

"Once your guy gets here, would you like to come inside?" she asked as the sound of a truck hummed toward them. Her gaze widened and he could almost hear her pulse pounding from here.

"I'm betting that is Hank. And I'll take you up on that offer," Griff said, hoping this would give him a reason to start a conversation with the town's most secretive resident.

Sure enough, the truck engine cut off and Hank came around the house a few moments later. Laurel's gaze, however, stayed glued to Griff. He gave a nod, and she exhaled.

"What do we have here?" Hank asked, cutting into the conversation between Griff and Laurel. He hoped the interruption didn't put her in the mood to be a hermit.

"I'll just be inside," she said, backing away like Hank might strike instead of the snake. There was a sudden chill in the air and Laurel looked like she couldn't get out of there fast enough.

"Be there in a few minutes, once this has been taken care of," Griff said to her, making eye contact and holding for a few seconds so she could gauge his sincerity.

Her smile was tentative, but not a rejection. He'd take the progress as he turned his attention back to Hank. He was as Texan as they come, oversized belt buckle included. He was also one of the nicest people Griff had ever met and he'd known the man since he was knee-high to a grasshopper.

"Water moccasin. At least one, and this baby is aggressive," he explained, glancing toward the house to see Laurel had closed her blinds. He put the fact in the 'not a good sign' column and kept moving. "I was almost struck. She's agitated and unpredictable."

"Let's see what we can find. I'll start by removing her," Hank said. He motioned toward the porch. "You might want to head over there and wait. The fewer people standing around as a threat, the better."

"Will do," Griff said, moving to the cabin and thinking how Laurel had looked almost as scared of Hank as she had the snake. As far as he knew, she lived here alone. Rumor had it she'd moved from a big city, but no one seemed to know a whole lot about her other than a few minor details. Most folks in these parts wore boots, whereas she wore shoes with low heels when she shopped at the grocery store, according to Sherry.

Had Laurel come to escape someone? Being in law enforcement, Griff's experience told him the biggest threat to a woman was her domestic partner. His hands fisted at his sides involuntarily at the thought. He'd come across it far too many times in his line of work and the anger he experienced never dulled. People who love each other should not physically or emotionally abuse one another. Period.

Griff flexed and released his fingers a few times to work off some of the anger. He redirected his thoughts to how he might ask Laurel questions casually, instead of sounding like an investigator who was grilling her to find out everything about her. He'd heard from previous dates that the kind of questions he asked out of curiosity could come across as interrogatory if he wasn't careful. He'd been told enough times for him to realize it was a problem, and probably a job hazard for someone who worked in law enforcement. He was a good investigator too, so that probably didn't help matters. This job could be twenty-four/seven, and impossible to turn off. Hence, the need for vacations he never had time to take.

Hank had wrangled the snake by the time Griff ended his thought.

"I'll secure this one in the truck and then we can search for others," Hank said. "No reason to worry about a nest, since Water Moccasins give live births. Wait for me to come back before you start. Okay?"

"Are you worried I'll find one first and take your job away?" Griff teased, trying to lighten the mood before heading inside in a few minutes.

"Go ahead and make my day," Hank said with a scowl. The man loved Clint Eastwood.

Griff chuckled. One of the reasons he loved living in Gunner was for characters like Hank.

After spending another fifteen minutes searching for any other hazards, Hank excused himself to relocate the snake while Griff walked toward the cabin. He knew the layout well, considering he'd been invited to parties out here at various stages of his young life. All the cabins were the same, coming in at roughly five hundred square feet. Each had a different color scheme. This particular cabin was yellow. Knowing these facts about the places in his hometown also made him very good at his job.

He tapped on the door three times. Nothing happened and there were no sounds coming from the other side. Did she reconsider her invitation? Was she inside hiding? More of those questions surfaced as he stood on the wooden porch. None he liked, because they all caused his mind to circle back to either abuse or trauma. In his professional experience, it was usually the former.

Having patience wasn't exactly in the job description of sheriff, but it sure helped that he had an abundance of it. Griff lifted his fist to knock again after another minute or two passed by. He couldn't be certain how much time had gone by, although it felt longer than it probably should have.

Using his knuckles, he rapped on the door again. This time he heard the creak of wood flooring underneath heavy footsteps. A few seconds later, the snick of the lock was followed by the door opening. Laurel's body blocked the entrance. She bit down on her bottom lip and, for a few seconds, looked like she was undecided about stepping back enough to allow him to enter.

Griff had encountered pretty much every type of person in his line of work; good, bad, and everything in between. He'd become decent at reading people based on the tension lines on their faces or the way they shifted weight from one foot to the other, signaling nervousness. Laurel was out of her comfort zone. Rather than push his luck, he offered a small smile.

"The snake has been taken care of," he said.

"Good," she said, blinking at him in a sure sign she was nervous. There were others, like her rapid breathing and the way her pulse pounded at the base of her throat.

This was going nowhere fast. He held up the empty bottle of water.

"Mind throwing this away?" he asked.

"Please, come inside," she said, opening the door wider before taking enough of a step back to allow him passage. "I apologize for my manners. I'm out of practice when it comes to having guests in my home."

"Not a problem," he said, before taking a step inside. The place was as he remembered, with enough bright yellow to make it seem like someone had bottled the sun and sprinkled it around.

"Have a seat." She held out a hand toward the small dining space. "Can I get you something else to drink?"

"No, thank you." He started toward the seat, then stopped. "Mind if I use your sink? I wouldn't mind washing my hands."

"You can use the bathroom," she offered. "Unless you want to wash your hands with dish soap. I'm out of the other kind in here."

"Will do," he said. He needed to figure out how to get her to open up to him soon. Time was ticking. At this rate, she would be asking him to leave before he could find out if she was safe. Asking her outright about her circumstances would only push her away and cause her to be even more protective. It could end up the equivalent of putting his hand out to an injured animal that had been cornered. Out of self-preservation, the animal would bite. When it got away, it wouldn't stop running.

Griff walked down the hallway, past the bedroom, and into the washroom. A bag of trash that had been tied off sat next to the small can. Trash day? A cabinet was left partially open. He glanced inside. The cabinet had been cleaned out. It was completely empty. He opened a couple of others, revealing the same.

Before Laurel could get suspicious, he turned on the spigot and pumped out a dab of foamy hand soap. After rubbing his hands together, he took note of the fact there was no bath towel hanging. He glanced around for something to use to dry his hands. Came up empty. Instead, he ended up patting them dry on his jeans.

The scene in the bathroom was suspicious. To make certain he was on track, he peeked behind the shower curtain. No soap and no shampoo. Not even a razor.

On the way back toward the living area, he glanced inside the bedroom. The door wasn't cracked much more than a sliver but he noticed the opened suitcase on top of the bed right away. Was Laurel in a hurry to go somewhere?

"I'm not sure I thanked you earlier for immediately charging to help after I screamed," she said as Griff re-entered the room.

"You're welcome, but it's muscle memory with a job like mine," he said with a half-smile. His attempt to put her at ease seemed to fail miserably, based on the small tension lines that formed when he referred to having a job. Interesting. He took note of the reaction and filed it in the back of his mind. He also realized he needed to think up a question or he'd be invited out the door. "How do you like living in Gunner so far?"

"It's great," she said with a forced smile. "This area is nice and the lake is beautiful."

"It's one of my favorite spots," he agreed.

"There's something magical about being on the water early in the morning," she continued, surprising him by continuing the conversation when he'd been almost certain the opposite was about to happen. There was a wistful quality to her eyes. A loneliness?

"Mind if I take you up on the earlier offer of a cup of coffee?" he asked. "Unless it would put you out."

"No," she quickly countered. "It's fine. I have one of those pod-thingies that makes a cup in like two seconds. It's no trouble at all. Why don't you take a seat and make yourself comfortable?"

Griff considered himself good at reading people. Laurel was packing up and getting ready to go. To move? It appeared so, based on the lack of bathroom products in the shower. In fact, he wondered if packing had been the reason she'd been delayed in answering the door. Surely, she didn't think someone had placed the snake there to intimidate her or run her off. Those snakes were rampant in Texas. It was only a matter of time before someone came face-to-face with them on the water. He was still scratching his head as to why she'd invited him in the second time, when she was clearly about to bolt.

Wasn't she happy here? Hadn't she found a place she could see herself calling home? As the questions mounted, Griff was more determined than ever to figure out what was going on with her. See if he could change her mind? Based on the suitcase, he didn't have a whole lot of time.

Or had she already reconsidered leaving? Was packing a knee-jerk reaction to her fear of the snake?

He needed to get her talking about something unimportant to put her at ease so he could wind up to bigger questions.

"I noticed you were bringing a kayak to the water earlier," he said.

"Right. I owe my landlord money to replace the oar after breaking it," she stated. "I hope he won't be angry about it. Just my luck it would be some irreplaceable family heirloom." She threw her hands in the air after pushing the button on the machine. It instantly fired up, spitting and sputtering until the glass coffee mug was full.

"I'm sure he'll understand. You acted in self-defense," Griff said. "Feel free to use me as a witness if it comes down to it."

"Do you think it will?" she asked.

The shock in her eyes and fear in her voice caused his chest to squeeze. His attempt to lighten the mood felt flat once again.

"No. I don't," he immediately reassured. "In fact, I know the owner of all the cabins around here and I can confidently say he would have told you to break the kayak if it meant saving yourself from a snakebite."

"Oh. Okay. Good," she said as she set down the mug in front of him.

"Are you joining me?" he asked.

"A cup of coffee is the last thing I need right now," she said, holding her hand out to show that it was still trembling.

Now, he really felt bad. His attempts at humor weren't working. Neither were his attempts at conversation in general. Griff wasn't normally so bad at this. Glancing around the cabin, he realized that not much had changed since the last time he was here. There were no personal items like photos on the fireplace mantel. The hand towels hanging over the oven door were the same ones he'd used before when he'd been inside manning the stove for a cookout. This place came fully furnished. He had expected little changes. It was missing those personal touches that made a space feel like home instead of a temporary stop.

So, where did he go from here?

CHAPTER THREE

"How about sitting down at least?"

The fact there was a stranger in Laurel's temporary home should probably have her ready to jump out of her skin. She nodded at his suggestion, thinking there were worse kinds of people to have around than a sheriff, when her stalker might have located her.

And, yes, it was most likely time to leave town. She'd started the packing process. Her year-long lease had been paid up in cash, which had been her suggestion and not the landlord's after he required a longer lease for the deadbolt. She hadn't wanted to leave more of a trail than she'd had to. The fake documents she'd secured through a connection from the 'disappearance' specialist she'd had lunch with, could be figured out if truly tested. She'd done the research to ensure her new place of employment was lax. That was the thing about moving out to the country; folks were trusting.

In the city, it was the complete opposite. Landlords checked credit scores, references, and past jobs. Her specialist had faked those too, but there was a price that came with using them. A financial cost that hit the account they'd helped her set up each time she used them. Staying hidden was more expensive than she realized and after nine months, she'd burned through a whole lot more of her cash than what she had coming in. She'd used paying her landlord up front and in cash as a negotiation tactic to lower the rent in addition to the added lock. At least, that was the excuse. He hadn't been too careful when he checked up on her, and her place of employment had been in need of employees.

Trust was something not easily given in the city. Here in Gunner, the opposite seemed to be true. It had been a refreshing change of pace. She'd bleached her hair blonde to hide the red. Thankfully, it had worked because getting dye to stick for a redhead was no small feat. Bleach was the great equalizer. At least her freckles had faded over the years.

"Have you lived here all your life?" she asked, turning the tables on the handsome sheriff before he could ask another question. Inviting him in, no matter how much having him here calmed her nerves, had been a mistake. She could see that now.

"I have," he said, subtly cocking an eyebrow before taking a sip of coffee. It seemed he was aware of the shift in tone.

"What about family?" she continued.

"I have a big one," he said as her gaze immediately dropped to the ring finger on his left hand. There was nothing there, not even a tan line. Did he choose not to wear a ring so criminals wouldn't know he was married?

Before the incident and trial, Laurel would never

have thought of people in terms of the secrets they kept. In fact, she had the basic belief that people were fundamentally honest. Her trust in people plummeted, and yet somewhere deep inside her wanted to believe in the good in humanity again. Life would be too awful without a little bit of hope to carry her through the dark times.

She must have given away her reaction because he added, "No wife and kids. I was talking about brothers and cousins."

"Oh," she said, before she could reign in the relief in her voice—relief she had no right to own. She'd been doing fine on her own. The thought of dating after having to defend herself from someone who was supposed to be in love with her had held little appeal. Then, there'd been the harassment from the cop.

Until now, she'd convinced herself that she'd lost faith in men, even though she knew a couple of bad seeds—even the really evil ones—didn't represent the entire gender. Feeling an attraction to the man sitting across from her at the table reminded her that she was still alive and capable of emotions. It was good. She hoped.

"How many do you have?"

"Four brothers and seven cousins," he admitted with a smile that transformed his face. "All boys."

"Wait a second," she said, mentally calculating the number. She'd seen some of the Quinns in town and they were all gorgeous men, but she had no idea there were...twelve altogether. "There's a dozen of you?"

"That's right," he said. "And before you say it, let me—"

"That's enough for a calendar," she cut him off midsentence.

He laughed a full-belly chuckle.

"I've heard that before," he said. As far as she was concerned, his looks stood far ahead of the others. And that was saying something considering how good-looking they were.

"Of course, you have," she said, trying to hide the red blush of embarrassment crawling up her neck. It always seemed to reach her cheeks where the color became all that much more concentrated. "Sorry."

"Don't apologize," he said, picking up his coffee mug and taking a sip. "I'm pretty sure some of the Quinns take it as the compliment it's meant to be."

"I guess telling you and your family that you're hot enough to sell calendars isn't too offensive," she said and her cheeks flamed. She really was stepping into it with the direction of this conversation. "Are you guys close?"

"All seven of my cousins either stayed to work the land at Quinnland or returned after my uncle brought them home for a big announcement," he said. "After a whole lot of anticipation, he turned over the ranch into their capable hands."

"And they were okay with everything?" she asked, finding that she wanted to learn more about Griff and his family. Or should she call him Sheriff Quinn? Laurel reminded herself not to get too comfortable around him. The last thing she needed was someone trained to notice the little things. She'd slipped a few times at Restful Acres, tiny little mistakes that no one other than Mrs. Brubaker seemed to catch onto. The great thing about most people was that they were usually too busy being lost in their own thoughts to really pay attention to details. Plus, if someone did call her on a mistake, she'd learned to play it off as a bad memory or suggest they'd heard wrong.

"They're all married now and starting their own traditions. Some already have kids, and they want them to grow up at Quinnland," he said, and there was a wistful quality to his voice.

She decided they didn't know each other well enough for her to ask for details. Plus, she had no idea what his family situation was. It was possible his side of the family owned part of the ranch.

"Did you always want to go into law enforcement?" she asked, figuring a change in topic might help. Also, she wanted to be the one asking questions instead of the other way around.

It was nice to talk to someone socially. She hadn't done that in longer than she cared to remember. Being on the run, making her way here while she stayed in pay-by-the-hour motels for six months had made her feel alone. She had a cell phone so she could get a job if need be along the way, and yet there were never any texts or calls. There was literally no one in the world who would know if she was still alive, because she'd had to break all ties when she'd disappeared in the middle of the night nine months ago. It had been tempting to stay in touch with her closest friend, but leaving a trail wasn't allowed if she wanted to stay hidden, according to the specialist. Her defense lawyer had called in a favor for the lunch.

For nine months, she made very little conversation with anyone. The isolation had been harder than she'd ever imagined. Leaving everything she'd known for most of her life was more difficult than she'd expected.

Being here in Gunner after slowly, methodically making her way down to Texas was the first thing that had felt right since the whole ordeal started. Laurel could scarcely wrap her mind around what had happened to cause her to walk away, and knew in her heart she could never look back. She involuntarily shivered at the memory that had been buried so deep it could only come out in nightmares. The escalation of actions and the family threats once the verdict came in, stating she had acted in self-defense. She'd believed this long and brutal nightmare would end after the jury trial, but it hadn't. The harassment almost immediately started. The threats. And it was her word against a cop's, so there was no winning there.

Him and the others were smart enough not to leave an evidence trail. The last straw had been when she realized someone had been inside her home when she wasn't there. She had no doubt in her mind someone had it out for her, and had been staking out her place. Had they come to figure out the best way to kill her and make it look like an accident? In her heart of hearts, the answer was a resounding yes. The same panic had gripped her today, as had gripped her when she'd discovered her drawers had been pilfered through. Nine months did nothing to lessen the fear and the wave of exhaustion that panic brought with it.

Bringing her concerns to the police chief hadn't done a whole lot of good. He'd expressed that tempers were running high but would eventually cool down. The brick with the word, *bitch,* written on it that had been thrown at the windshield of her parked car at the grocery store was just overzealous teenagers. Chief Russo had told her to sit tight and the whole mess would blow over in a couple of weeks.

Livid beyond words, she'd walked out of his office with the clear knowledge he wasn't going to do a whole lot to investigate the crimes. The last thing she'd asked him was whether or not he would step in if someone tried to kill her.

The man who'd been sworn to protect and to serve had stared at her with cold, dark eyes long enough to make her want to climb out of her own skin. Then, he'd said, "I'll do what I can. However, bear in mind this community lost one of its sons, and neither me nor my cops can be everywhere at all times."

The threat had sent a cold chill racing down her spine.

Glancing up, looking into Griff's eyes, she saw the exact opposite of Russo. First of all, the two couldn't be more different. Griff had to be six-feet-four-inches at a minimum, and yet he moved with the grace of an athlete in the zone.

She also realized he was studying her.

"I think I'll have that cup of coffee now," she said by way of excuse as she fumbled to push off the table and nearly ended up splayed out on the floor on her backside. If not for Griff's fast reflexes, she would have ended up splat on the rug. He grabbed her elbow in time to steady her. His touch was electric and exciting rolled into one, and something that took her breath away.

Blinking a couple of times after righting herself, she thanked him and headed over to the kitchen.

"How long do you plan to stay in Gunner?" Griff asked.

Laurel hated liars and refused to be one. For the most part, she could sidestep when posed with an uncomfortable question rather than outright lie. Her hesitation in answering probably gave her away.

"I haven't decided," she finally said as she popped in the pod and then bit back a yawn. By this point, on a normal day, she would probably be in the shower by now. Since she was going to have a long day ahead packing and then slipping out of town, she needed the caffeine boost.

"Not putting down roots?" he continued.

She shrugged noncommittally.

"I really like my job," she said, then it hit her like a ton of bricks out of the sky. She couldn't leave town without saying goodbye to Mrs. Brubaker. The woman with eyes that reminded Laurel of the grandmother who'd taken her in and brought her up despite being on a fixed income. Her heart suddenly cramped.

She had to find a way to stop by Restful Acres to say goodbye. Mrs. Brubaker was the first person who made Laurel feel welcome in Gunner and like, maybe, the world wasn't ending after all. The spunky older woman was important to Laurel.

Laurel was running out of steam on the 'pack up and bolt out of town' idea. Could she stick around a couple more days?

———

Griff took his time sipping his coffee, figuring this might be the last chance he got to spend time with Laurel before she left. Her intentions were crystal clear to him at this point, get out of Dodge. A moment of sadness crept in at the loss of chance to get to know her. He'd become good at sizing people up in a hurry. In fact, his life could depend on it, so he paid attention.

Instinct and experience said there was so much more to Laurel than a beautiful outer shell. Although, that was as close to perfect as he could imagine anyone being. The freckle just above her top lip on the right side of her mouth begged to be kissed. But he'd learned a long time ago that beauty could fade the minute someone opened their mouth and spoke. Intelligence was far sexier. A sense of humor was important and only added to someone's appeal. He had a sneaky suspicion that behind those weary blue eyes was a formidable brain and someone who, at least at one time, knew how to crack a joke.

Laurel didn't join him back at the table. Instead, she turned around and leaned a slender hip against the bull-nose edge of the granite counter. This was a bad sign for further conversation. It meant she was ready for him to go.

Reluctantly, he took a final sip of coffee and then pushed to standing.

"I'd better head out," he said, walking over to the sink.

"Okay," she said, sounding a little startled at the abruptness of his gesture. He was just beating her to the punch. Besides, waiting until she gave him the heave-ho would only put her on guard more than she already was.

It wasn't his intention to make her uncomfortable in her own home, temporary as the place might be.

As it was, he was going to have to write Laurel Roberts off for good as a missed opportunity to get to know someone instinct said he was going to like.

He rinsed out his coffee cup and set it inside the sink to the backdrop of her protests.

"I can take care of that," she said, placing her hand on his forearm. No touch should feel this electric and body altering.

Griff hadn't experienced this level of chemistry in far too long.

He glanced down at the point of contact and then lifted his gaze to meet hers. There was so much chemistry firing between them that he was momentarily frozen in time while trying to figure out what was going on with his body.

An attraction this explosive couldn't be good for either one of them. She had looked ready to bolt at any moment, like a deer that had picked up the scent of a hunter, for the entire time he'd been in her cabin. Now?

Her blue eyes darkened with something that looked a whole lot like need. There were other signals that should have clued him in to what was about to happen. Yet, nothing prepared him for her pressing up to her tiptoes and kissing him.

Her full lips against his brought out a low groan from deep in his chest. This wasn't the time or place to put too much stock into what was happening. He'd studied this before. She was most likely seeking proof of life, and this was nothing more than biology kicking in.

So, he pulled back first.

"Not a good idea," was all he managed to say while trying to slow his breathing. The second her lips had touched his, his pulse had skyrocketed.

"You are so right and that is not like me. I'm so sorry," she said, and her cheeks flushed bright red with what looked like embarrassment. Rather than sink into humiliation like he was used to seeing people do in similar situations, she took in a breath and seemed to force her shoulders back. "Won't happen again."

Griff needed to set the record straight. Fast. "As much as I would very much like it to happen for the right reasons, that's not what we're dealing with here." He figured this was the time to put a few cards on the table. "I couldn't help noticing the emptied-out shelves in the bathroom even though I promise I was only there to wash my hands. Which leads me to a serious question that I'm hoping you'll answer. Are you leaving town?"

Laurel bit down on her bottom lip like she was trying to physically force herself to slow down and think before she spoke. A few seconds ticked by as a multitude of emotions passed over her face. It gave him the impression she hadn't made up her mind about whether or not she should stick around. Where she lived and if she disappeared from Gunner forever wasn't his business, except there was that look of fear in her eyes and the fact she looked ready to jump at the slightest noise. Letting her leave now without trying to convince her to stay and let him help her, seemed like he might be throwing her directly into the lion's den.

If there truly was a threat and she was running from something, it would eventually catch up to her. She seemed to know it too. And yet this didn't seem like the right moment to remind her of the fact.

Finally, she issued a sharp sigh and then locked gazes with him.

"To be honest, I'm going back and forth on whether or not it's time to go," she admitted.

"I can be a good person to bounce ideas off of if you want to talk to someone about the decision. Go over the pluses and minuses," he said, thinking this was the most she'd said about her personal life so far.

She nodded while looking up and to the right. The good news was that she was seriously considering his offer. The not-so-great part was he couldn't tell which way she was going. Or what he could say to convince her to stick around. The connection he felt with her was something that normally took time to build. Theirs had been instant.

Call it chemistry or whatever, but he hadn't experienced a pull like this in longer than he cared to remember. Of course, working long days and nights keeping his county safe was a huge responsibility and one he didn't take lightly. At thirty-four, he was young for the job he'd held since his thirtieth birthday. And yet, law enforcement had been a way of life in his family. Two of his brothers worked for the U.S. Marshal Service. The two sides of the family ended up cattle ranchers and law enforcement. Who would have guessed? Their feuding fathers seemed to do everything possible to draw lines between the family.

"I'm not sure," Laurel cut into his thoughts. She took a step back and then picked up her coffee mug, rolling it between her palms. Her gaze dropped to the ground like the answer might be written there.

"I just thought you should know what your options are," he said. "I already said I'm a good listener. Anything you tell me can be kept confidential, unless there's a crime involved."

Her eyebrow shot up at the last part of his sentence. Had he just erased all the goodwill he'd worked so hard to gain during this conversation?

"And to be clear, I mean that *you* specifically committed a crime," he clarified. "Not a crime in general terms, or something that has been committed against you. In that case, I can only remind you of your rights, and hope that you'll give me a good reason for not taking action to put a criminal away so he can't hurt someone else."

Griff had dealt with every type of person during his time as sheriff. He'd heard stories from his father, who'd had the job even before him. All the experience and interactions gave him a good feel for people beyond just a gut instinct. Based on the vibe he'd received from Laurel so far, there was no doubt in his mind she was a good person. The few folks in town who'd done business with her had nothing but good things to say about the new resident. He believed he would have heard something derogatory about her by now. She'd been in town three months already.

Was there anything he could say to influence her decision to stick around for a fourth?

CHAPTER FOUR

Laurel was teetering on a ledge. On the one hand, she hadn't really talked to an actual person in a social setting in almost three years since the very early days of the ordeal. And conversation with Griff came as easily as breathing. Her talks with Mrs. Brubaker were a lifeline and mainly centered around the older woman, her past, and the amazing life she'd lived. They were also work related. Laurel had to check on her patients and see how they were doing, but Laurel rarely ever shared anything personal and never spoke of her past. In a way, having to be secret about something so traumatic made her feel victimized all over again. She didn't even feel safe seeking counseling even though she was well aware of patient–therapist confidentiality. There was always that lingering doubt if the counselor would know someone from the family and word would somehow get back to them of Laurel's whereabouts. The thought of the harassment starting all over again caused the air in the room to thin and her chest to squeeze.

Cory Stapleton, her lawyer, had advised her to keep quiet after an assault that had had her fighting for her own life. She had yet to unpack the trauma caused by being alone in a room with a man after. And yet, here she was inviting Griff inside her cabin, not wanting him to leave.

During the trial, a judge had ordered her to only speak to her attorney and a counselor about the details of the high-profile case. The assault wouldn't have made national news, and yet it had been huge in the area she lived.

After the trial and her acquittal, no one would talk to her except her best friend, Marissa Jones. Her friend had young twins and no family help. As much as Marissa had wanted to be there for Laurel for every step, life got in the way. There was no way Laurel would ask to come first over her godbabies.

Then there was the fact Laurel had a difficult time looking at, much less speaking with, anyone in law enforcement after the way she'd been treated. On some level, she realized how unfair it was to blame Griff Quinn for sins he didn't commit. There were good and bad people in every job, every walk of life, and every neighborhood. After having her trust violated to the degree she'd experienced, trusting anyone with a badge was going to be difficult.

Griff was tall, muscled, and looked like he could take care of himself and anyone else around in the process. He had sandy-blond hair, a chiseled from granite jawline, and the most incredible pair of honey-brown eyes. The man was perfection.

There was something about the sheriff's demeanor that put her at ease.

It was difficult to explain and even harder to understand given what she'd been through. He had an air of honor and fairness that she couldn't quite pinpoint. There was so much confidence in the way he carried himself. It probably didn't hurt that he was from Texas, and the knowledge he'd been brought up in a ranching family where values like honor and keeping someone's word still meant something to people.

Cattle ranchers were some of the hardest workers and most humble people she'd ever met. Was it the fact they took care of animals and the land that caused them to be so down to earth? Was it the constant knowledge they were at the whim of Mother Nature that made them never forget how little control they had in life? Or was it the combination of all those things stirred in one big pot that seemed to turn out more good people than not?

"Can I ask you a question?" Griff cut into her thoughts. There was a spark in his coffee-colored eyes that drew her toward him and made her want to lean into him.

She nodded.

"What are you doing for the rest of today?" he asked, the moment of uncertainty in his eyes tugged at her heartstrings.

Should she answer him honestly? Half an hour ago she'd been certain she would be packed and on the road before her third cup of coffee had time to kick in. Now? She didn't want to leave Gunner forever without stopping by to say goodbye to Mrs. Brubaker. It didn't seem right to leave this way, slinking out of town like she was the criminal. She still had no real evidence anyone had broken into her home in Chicago to set a trap for her, except that she *knew*.

"I should probably clean house," she said, basically code for gather the rest of her things and get out while she was still alive. But then no one had moved from behind the tree when she could have sworn she'd seen a shadow earlier. Was her imagination playing tricks on her?

Between the shadow, Henry, and the snake, Laurel's nerves were fried. Except Griff Quinn had a calming effect on her. Would it be a mistake to run away from Gunner, from him?

"Or you could accompany me to a festival today," he offered.

"I don't think that's a good—"

"Think about it," he said as he fished a small black leather wallet out of his back pocket. He extracted a business card and then set it on the counter. "My number is on there. I need to go home and get cleaned up. Then, I'm heading out to the festival. I'd like to take you there and show you how incredible the people of this town can be and what a great place Gunner is. But no pressure. If you want me to come back and pick you up, text the number on the card. If you get confirmation from me, that means the text came through. If not, you might have to call. Either way, I promise not to be offended."

Griff Quinn thanked her for the coffee and then walked out the front door, pausing long enough to remind her to lock it behind him.

She did, and then she stood at the door like a teenager who'd just been dropped off by her high school crush. Heart beating erratically in her chest, pounding the inside of her ribcage, she let out the breath she'd been holding.

On the one hand, she wondered how much it could hurt to stick around for another day. Constantly being on the run like in the first nine months of the year had been exhausting. After three months of anonymity, she was just beginning to feel safe in her own skin again. The need to constantly look over her shoulder had diminished somewhat, and she could see a time when she would almost feel normal again in the not so distant future. She woke up in the middle of the night in a cold sweat less often.

What happened to her after the death was horrible. The harassment was unthinkable. Being responsible for someone's death, despite acting in self-defense, caused tremors and night terrors for the two years following the incident. The trial was traumatizing but she'd refused to see herself as a victim even when the prosecutor had done her best to discredit Laurel. Go down that road and she might never recover.

Besides, the death really had been an accident on her part. She hadn't set out to cause the loss of someone's life, especially not someone she believed she cared for at one time. Had she been naïve to think her ex would change when she'd brought up his temper? Absolutely.

Looking back, there'd been red flags early on in the relationship, but he'd been charming too. So charming, in fact, that she didn't even realize how much she was making excuses for his other behaviors. To be fair, he'd concealed them well from her and had showered her with attention in the early months of dating. Laurel didn't have a ton of dating experience to draw on for comparison. She'd worked her way through high school to be less of a burden on the grandmother who'd raised her. She'd put herself through two years of community college, graduating with an associate's degree in communication. Laurel had had no idea what she wanted to be, so basic business courses had seemed like a good idea. Once she'd decided on a major, nursing, her grandmother had become sick.

For the next three years, Laurel had stayed by her grandmother's side when not working. Her associate's degree didn't go far in the small suburb where they lived. She'd planned to move to the city after completing a nursing degree. Funny, she'd never told her ex about her hopes and dreams.

Timothy had been her fourth boyfriend, if she excluded Christopher from high school. They'd 'dated' senior year if she could even call it that. But he'd been sweet enough to carry her books for her and meet her at the door of her classroom. He'd been on the wrestling team and spent most of his nights and weekends with school athletics or studying. They'd never even kissed. It wasn't until six months after their breakup during freshman year that he 'came out' while at the University of Chicago.

The news explained a lot about their platonic relationship. Granted, she wasn't ready to do anything physical with a boy in high school. But it explained why Christopher had never even attempted to kiss her on the lips. A quick peck on the cheek was as far as the two of them had gotten.

Once news broke, he'd sent her an apology via text, stating that he really had loved her in his own way. She'd smiled, realizing he'd been a safe choice for a high school boyfriend on her part and she seemed to be the same for him. They'd started as friends and probably should have stayed in the lane.

Reminiscing about her past was one thing. Her present stared her in the face, calling for a decision as to whether or not she planned to finish packing up the few belongings she had or stick around.

Glancing around, it was sad to realize just how little anything belonged to her. There was something deep in her soul that wanted to put down roots in a place that felt like home. Chicago had been good to her, or maybe it was just her grandmother who'd made it feel like warmth and apple pie.

Once her grandmother had passed away, the feeling of being all alone in the world without family had engulfed her. Marissa had married almost straight out of high school, changing the dynamic of their friendship. For obvious reasons, building a life with her new husband had to come first. Max was a decent guy. Him and Marissa had been high school sweethearts who seemed like they would go the distance. At the time of their marriage, the summer after graduation, Laurel had been skeptical. Then she realized those two had something most couples didn't seem to find...respect for each other. It wasn't until she ended her short-lived relationship with Timothy that she realized how important respect was between two people who were supposed to care about each other. Timothy had been all dazzle and charm, a front for a monster. Even though it hadn't taken her long to realize he wasn't what he had seemed, he'd locked on.

She shivered at remembering his last words to her. *You belong to me. I say when we're done.*

Then, he'd tried to rape her.

Laurel pushed off the counter's edge and paced. There'd been so much blood when he fell on the knife, the knife that he'd been holding against her throat as he forced her clothes off. The small scar marked her, reminded her.

Somehow, she'd managed to spin out of his grip when he got distracted. He'd taken his eyes off her face for a split second, licking his lips as his gaze dropped to her chest.

Everything had happened in slow motion at the time, as if time had slowed to a standstill. Memories now were vague. However, there were a couple of things she would never forget. The look on his face when he told her exactly what he was going to do to her next. The anger in his eyes that could only be described as pure evil. The saying about the eyes being the window to the soul resonated with her.

Griff Quinn couldn't be more different; the complete antithesis to everything she'd experienced with Timothy. Even from afar, she'd sensed his calm presence.

It was odd to her how she seemed to know when he walked into a room. It was also easy to see that she wasn't the only one who seemed to have radar tuned to him. All the female cashiers at the grocery store perked up just a bit more, many of them suddenly felt the need to check their lipstick in the mirror or finger comb their hair. The pruning began the second he was out of sight. The switch to when he returned was just as obvious. They all tried their hardest to make it seem like they had no idea he was around.

Did he realize what was going on around him? Because it didn't come across that he noticed one way or another. The fact had made her crack a smile when she saw all the shoulders sag once he left the building. The only person left smiling was the line he'd been in.

Laurel laughed, despite the earlier heavy thoughts. Griff Quinn held a special kind of magic. The funny part was that he didn't seem to know or care. Now that she really thought about it, a man paid to notice others couldn't possibly have missed the antics going on around him. Then again, maybe he was so used to it that it no longer registered. Maybe he would be more thrown off by walking into a room without being noticed.

It struck Laurel that the man she barely knew was taking up so much of her thoughts. Was she that desperate for company? She glanced at the business card sitting on the counter. Or was there something special about the sheriff?

———

Griff's journey from the cabin to the boat to his truck seemed to take longer than usual. The number of times he'd glanced at his phone wasn't helping time pass any quicker. If anything, he was much more aware of every passing minute.

The excuse he'd sold himself was that he'd been away from work too long today and Sherry might need him. Except that a voice deep in the back of his mind refused to accept the lie. The voice of reason?

Call it whatever, but the voice was annoying as all get-out. Walking away from Laurel had been the right thing to do. If she was going to leave town, there wasn't much he could do to stop her. So, why did that same voice in the back of his mind think it was a good idea to remind him of all the things he hadn't said that he probably should have? Like she could call him anytime day or night, if she was scared or felt threatened in any way. All those unspoken words seemed to jumble up in his thoughts, leave him unsettled and with a sense of unfinished business.

Then there was the bigger question of why he seemed to care so much about whether or not a practical stranger stayed in Gunner or moved as far away as possible. It wasn't like he was desperate for company and she wasn't exactly the most talkative person, even though silence between them hadn't been awkward.

From what he'd gathered after hearing town folk talk about the resident beauty, Laurel was a nice person. The whole reason he got into law enforcement in the first place was to deliver justice to those who'd been wronged. As Pollyanna as it all sounded, he wanted to make a difference. No, *needed* to make a difference. There was something deep inside Griff that made him want to run toward danger if it meant saving another's life. He couldn't explain it. Although, a psychiatrist

worth his or her salt would probably track it back to
not being able to save his own mother.

Griff didn't care where the deep-seated desire came
from. All he knew was helping others when they'd experienced the worst day of their life, or locking away
someone preying on decent people helped him sleep
better at night. The fact two of his other brothers had
gone into law enforcement said there must be something in their blood. These kinds of jobs seemed to run
in families, he'd noticed. Did they inherit a different
type of wiring? Possibly. The reason didn't matter.

Instead, there he was, feeling helpless since Laurel
seemed determined not to talk about her past—a past
that had her packing up and ready to run away without
a word.

Griff sighed, trying to shake off the failure as he
navigated out of the parking lot of the lake. A question
nagged him. Would he ever see Laurel again?

Another one joined it. Was Laurel even her real
name? He could admit his curiosity about her was more
than professional. There was a personal draw that made
him want to turn his truck around and head toward the
cabin. Making a U-turn wouldn't be too complicated,
and he could be back at her front door within the hour.
He could make an excuse about thinking he'd left his
cell phone, so he could check on her.

Griff shook his head and continued toward home
instead. Back at his place, he figured he could grab a
quick shower and change his clothes before heading
over to check out the festival. His mood had soured, so
he needed cheering up. The three-day event would open
in a couple of hours. The organizers always brought

their own security who did a standup job. It was Griff's night to attend as a civilian. He would be 'on' tomorrow, despite his deputies telling him not to worry. They had it covered; Deputy Hernandez planned to work all three nights.

The cell beside him buzzed and hope filled his chest. Until he glanced at the screen and realized it was Hernandez on the line.

"Griff here. What's up?" he immediately asked as a sense of dread filled him. If anything was going south with the event, wouldn't Sherry have been the one to call?

"Hey, boss," Hernandez started, his tone of voice already calming Griff's nerves. Law enforcement officers trained themselves to listen for the slightest inflection to determine if one of their co-workers needed assistance. The tension in Griff's shoulders relaxed. "How many did you catch?"

"None," Griff admitted, thinking just how far that answer stretched. "Why? What's up?"

"Touching base with you about the festival. Just wanted you to know that Sayer and I have everything under control on our part. We're working with their security detail, as always, and everything is looking copasetic."

Hernandez loved referencing the 1970s, despite being born twenty years later. He said he'd been born in the wrong decade and preferred the disco era to the music that wasn't even music today they liked to call rap.

"Sounds good. All communications systems are in place, I take it," Griff said, curious as to why his deputy would make a call and not actually say anything of importance. These kinds of check-ins weren't the norm.

"We got it all set up and ready to go," Hernandez informed.

"There will be a lot of out-of-towners breezing through over the next couple of days. I already felt it in traffic on the way home from the lake," Griff pointed out, thinking out loud.

"Yes, there will be, and hopefully this will bring in some much needed revenue to some of our local shop owners after having a rough year," Hernandez said. The festival was a really great way to bring in people to buy locally made jewelry, arts, and crafts, and folks stopped in restaurants to get a break from festival food or on their way home. It helped everyone in their little community.

"Is Ms. Meyer selling those more of those 'redneck' wine glasses?" Griff asked on a chuckle.

"Last I checked, she sure planned to. I don't know why those things are popular but you already know my girlfriend bought a dozen last fall," Hernandez said, sounding every bit as confused and bewildered by the purchase, as he had when he'd announced that he needed a box to take them home last year.

"They worked out okay at the annual community caregiver picnic," Griff pointed out.

"I mean, I didn't hear anybody talking about those," Hernandez said. "Now, my brisket...that was something. People couldn't stop talking about how amazing it was."

"It was a little less dry this year," Griff teased, knowing full well he was poking the bear with the off-handed comment. Hernandez took a whole lot of pride in his grilling skills. At least this conversation was putting Griff in a lighter mood after his conversation with Laurel. The fearful look in her eyes, despite her show of strength, would haunt him for days.

"I know you did not just insult my meat grilling skills," Hernandez said in about as disgusted and put-off voice as Griff had ever heard from his deputy.

"I'm just saying, it could have been a little less dry," Griff continued to tease.

"Do I hear a challenge in there somewhere?" Hernandez asked, not one to back away from competition. "Because you know I will bring it even more next year..."

"I don't see how I can lose in that bet," Griff said. "I either get better brisket, or bragging rights for days. Basically, a win-win for me. So, yeah, I dare you to make a more tender brisket next summer."

"Next summer?" Hernandez said with indignance, continuing the banter. "We are about to have brisket for Thanksgiving, and you're invited."

It was good to see his deputy was healed and doing well after being shot on duty, a little more than a year ago.

"Oh, I see how you're playing it now. You're poking the bear. No, you're talking to a master here. I do not accept your insults and I will not be manipulated," Hernandez feigned disgust like no one else could.

"In all seriousness, though. It's good to hear everything is looking good for the festival. Staff is all up and raring to go," Griff stated. He pulled in front of his home and needed to park. Reversing into his drive, so that he could deposit his boat and trailer into the one-

car garage, required every bit of his concentration skills
to tuck the trailer and boat into their place.

"So, there was another reason for my call,"
Hernandez hedged. Something was up.

"Okay?"

"You know Becca," Hernandez began. The fact that
he seemed to need to choose his words correctly did
not send a whole lot of warmth and fuzzies through
Griff.

"Yes, we've met. Why? What is going—"

"Before you say no, I told Becca that I would at least
ask if you were interested," Hernandez said.

"I don't need to be fixed up," Griff said. "I'm doing
fine on my own, thank you very much."

Griff ended the call thinking if that statement was
true, he wouldn't be attending the festival alone. His
thoughts shifted back to Laurel and how unfortunate it
was for him that the first interesting person to come to
town in ages was probably already on the highway
heading as far away from him and the town of Gunner
as she could get.

CHAPTER FIVE

Laurel was having a record-setting bad day. First, the shadow behind the tree at Restful Acres had startled her. Secondly, Henry, her neighborhood feral cat had scared the bejesus out of her the minute she'd returned home after her shift. Then, a water moccasin had come at her as she was dragging her kayak toward the water. She could only pray the rule of three applied here and the worst had already happened to her. To think that this was a foreshadowing of how the next few days was going to go, was too depressing.

To make matters worse, she'd not only invited the town's drop-dead gorgeous sheriff inside her home but she'd kissed him. She was still scratching her head over how she'd decided that that would be a good idea.

Pacing around her kitchen, she'd gotten more than enough steps in for an entire week. She'd been circling the small space, trying to figure out what had motivated her to kiss a man she barely knew. Was she that desperate? Was she that lonely? Was he that good looking?

At least she knew the answer to the last question. Yes. Griff Quinn was the entire package; good looks, intelligence, and an intensity that made her want to go to him and tell him all about her past. There was something about the tall cowboy sheriff that made her want to lean into his strength. There was something about being around someone who she could trust not to let her down, at least not knowingly. And there was something about being with a person who could take care of himself.

She had been aware of his presence over the last three months and had intentionally kept enough distance between them to block any of his natural ability to draw all the attention in the room. The man seemed trustworthy and part of her wanted to confide in someone and really talk. She'd kept all the details of her past locked up inside her, hidden, even from Mrs. Brubaker. And there was a question she failed to have an answer to...how long could she continue to live like this?

Laurel reminded herself to give it more time. It had only been nine months since she'd left everything familiar, to slowly make her way down to Gunner.

She stared at the one-inch by two-inch glossy card that was still sitting on her countertop. All she had to do was walk over to the table where she'd left her cell phone, pick it up, and make the call. A very large part of her wanted to do just that. Why did Griff Quinn have to be law enforcement?

Laurel walked into the adjacent room, her bedroom, and plopped down on the bed. Hands clasped in her lap, she glanced around at the single dresser and the closet that was barely big enough for her to step inside and turn around in. All of her clothing fit inside one dresser and one small closet, and that was all she'd brought with her. She hadn't even had time to pack up her old space, or rent a storage unit. She kept a small metal box with a couple of papers from her grandmother, mostly keep-sakes like her grandmother's birth certificate and driver's license from the nineties. Her grandmother had kept a little prayer card in her wallet. The card had been laminated and all the edges were worn. Her grand-mother had said the prayer on the card always offered comfort and protection.

She'd given the card to Laurel 'for safe keeping' at Laurel's high school graduation. They'd taken a picture together that day that had always sat on her nightstand. It was one of her most prized possessions.

Here, it was too risky to leave any identifiers around. The person who'd broken into her Chicago apartment could track her down here. Or so the reloca-tion specialist had pointed out. So, it was best to leave the cabin as a blank canvas with nothing to prove one way or the other that she lived here. When she'd asked the specialist how long she would need to stay away, and how much time would need to pass before the grudges died down and something else replaced her as news, the answer had knocked the wind out of her. Years.

Laurel had no idea how anyone could hate another person so much and hold onto that hatred not for days, not for weeks, not even for months. But for *years*. She realized that she had taken a life. She was painfully aware of the fact. She also acknowledged that she'd had no choice at the time. It had been a horrible accident born out of self-defense. She'd been naïve about the fact people would automatically be on her side. She'd believed surely once the details came out during the trial that folks would see Timothy as the evil person he became and understand her side. Possibly even try to comfort her because the act of taking another life even by self-defense left a mark that she wasn't sure she could ever recover from.

Needless to say, people had shocked the heck out of her. The fact so many had commented what a great family Timothy had come from, and what an amazing family he'd left behind, when those statements couldn't be further from the truth, was still a knife to the chest.

Shame on them.

Despite their rejection, she refused to give in to the dark cloud that seemed to follow her and try to engulf her in the two years from the incident to the final, exonerating jury verdict. In those two years, she'd been unable to work and unable to leave town. The horror of being arrested on the scene when she'd been victimized would live in her thoughts forever. At this point, the only thing she truly missed was Marissa and the twins. Marissa's husband had been a champion and had taken more than a little heat when he'd allowed her to stay at their house, when she couldn't go home right away after being detained and 'released pending further investigation.'

Enough. Laurel made up her mind right then to get up and get out. She felt herself falling down that sink-hole of regret and confusion and sadness. And she knew just the thing to distract herself and quite possibly cheer herself up.

Griff was stepping out of the shower when he heard his cell phone buzz in the next room. He quickly jumped into action, wrapping a towel around his waist as he shook his head like a wet dog trying to shake water out of his wavy, but short hair.

One more ring and the call would go into voicemail, so he picked up the pace. His phone sat on top of his bed, right where he left it. He glanced at the screen and saw the unknown number. This was his personal cell which he didn't really give out other than Sherry, his family, his deputies, and those he knew personally. This wasn't his public line. For a split second, he almost considered not answering, because the last thing he needed was another offer for an extended warranty on his truck or any other sales pitch for that matter.

But curiosity got the best of him, or perhaps it was just wishful thinking, and he answered.

"Hello?" He did his best to hide the slight edge of irritation in his voice. Then again, this call could be coming from anyone, except that Sherry normally only patched through anything work-related.

"Did I catch you at a bad time?" the female voice asked. He recognized it instantly. Laurel. His heart did a little dance. Then he remembered he'd given her the card with his personal cell. The ones he only gave out to folks he thought might need a direct line to him.

"No. Not at all," he reassured. "In fact, I was just getting out of the shower and was about to get dressed to head on over to the festival."

It occurred to him she might be in some other form

of danger, like another snake or a poisonous spider. Or worse. His chest deflated a little at the thought the call might not be for personal reasons.

"Everything okay?" he asked.

"Okay is probably a relative term considering I kissed a complete stranger today, but, yes, I'm okay," she said, and he could hear the tentativeness in her voice. And the embarrassment. "But if your offer still stands to go to the festival together, I can be ready by the time you swing by and pick me up."

"It's a date," he said, trying to hide the shock in his voice. He cleared his throat, hoping it would create a distraction, and continued, "My place is probably twenty-five minutes from your side of the lake. I need another five to finish dressing. How about I plan to pick you up in half an hour?"

"I'll be ready," she said, when he feared she might find a way to back out instead. To be fair, she was the one who'd done the calling. He'd done it that way on purpose because he wanted her to feel in control of the next step. It was up to her to call or walk away.

Griff thanked her before ending the call, and was a little lighter in his step. An excitement and anticipation filled him that he hadn't felt in ages. Laurel was a true mystery, and he was happy that she had decided to stick around. At least for today. Then again, maybe she needed to pick up a paycheck before she could go or some other reason that had nothing to do with him.

Either way, he wouldn't look a gift horse in the mouth. He chunked his cell phone on top of the bedspread, and made quick work of throwing on boxers, a fresh pair of jeans, and a collared button-down shirt along with clean socks.

As promised, he was out the door in roughly five minutes after running a brush through his hair and throwing on a Stetson. He beat his own time making it to her cabin in a solid twenty-three minutes. Living in the same town for all of his life had made him very good at knowing how long it would take him to get somewhere. More often than not, he was able to find a way to shave off a minute or two here and there based on traffic.

As he cut off the truck engine and threw his shoulder into the door to open it, the front door swung open. His heart skipped a couple of beats when he got a good look at Laurel and saw the nervous shine in her eyes. She had on a coral-colored western minidress that brushed her leg midthigh along with tan and teal cowgirl boots. The top of her dress was a half-moon that showed just enough of her creamy skin, without giving away much more than a hint of the full breasts beneath the material.

Griff did his best to catch his breath as he bolted around the front end of his truck and over to the passenger side to open the door for her. For a brief moment, they locked eyes.

"You take my breath away," he said to Laurel. "You're beautiful."

"Thank you," she said quietly with an expression that made him feel like he'd caught her off guard with the compliment. Her cheeks turned a darker shade of pink and he realized that seemed to be her go-to reaction when she was embarrassed. Someone as beautiful as her should be very used to being complimented but that wasn't how this situation was reading.

It surprised him that she didn't seem to be comfortable with it. He made a mental note as he closed the truck door behind her and then came around the front of his vehicle. A few seconds later, he reclaimed the driver's seat, taking note of just how much his throat had dried up since that front door had opened and Laurel had emerged.

"Where do you hail from?" Griff asked as he cranked the engine. He put the gearshift into reverse, backed out of the drive, and then navigated onto the dirt road leading to the main drive toward the festival.

"From the Midwest," she said, and he noticed she kept her answer purposely vague.

He was making small talk, not especially trying to drill her for information. So the fact that she wanted to be with him, since she was the one who'd made the call, but was also so guarded about the details of her life and her past told him to tread lightly. The last thing he wanted to do was spook her again.

Besides, she'd made the decision to stick around at least for another day. And he hoped in the next couple of hours to give her reason to stay tomorrow too.

———

The smell of spice and outdoors mixed with sandalwood filled Laurel's senses in the cab of the pickup truck that was remarkably clean, for someone who was related to cattle ranchers. Granted, Griff was the town's sheriff, but she made the mental leap that he went out onto the property, and probably even pitched in when needed. He seemed like the kind of person who'd do just that, if he had a day off. After all, he'd spent this one rescuing her from a snake.

"Thank you, by the way," she said to him, realizing she hadn't said those words earlier in the day when she'd meant to.

"For?" he asked. The fact he seemed genuinely confused about where she was going with this endeared him to her even more. He also seemed like the kind of person who lived by a cowboy code of honor and not giving his word unless he meant it. There was something incredibly sexy about that right now in her life.

She also needed to steer the conversation in a new direction because giving up personal details of her past life wasn't about to happen.

"This morning. For racing over to help when you heard me screaming like a wild woman on the shore," she continued.

"It nothing. I was glad to help," he said.

"It wasn't 'nothing' to me," she stated. "Looking back, I panicked and probably scared the snake a whole lot more by smacking at it with the oar. I'm not exactly going to call it a poor thing, but it was just doing what came naturally to it."

"That one was aggressive," he said. "You were right to have the reaction you did. You might have saved yourself a trip to the ER. Those buggers can be nasty when they want to be."

"I was just thinking maybe it was a mom protecting her babies," she said. "Aren't snakes a whole lot more dangerous when they nest?"

"Yes, but this particular breed has live births, so there was no reason for it to be aggressive, other than just being onery and the fact you may have surprised it," he explained.

Good to know that in addition to an entire town, she'd offended a snake just by her presence as well.

"What kind of festival are we going to?" She figured it was a safer question. Changing the subject from personal questions to their evening in town would make her a whole lot more comfortable on this ride.

"I'm surprised you haven't heard about it," Griff said.

"Guess I've been locked in my own world," she admitted.

"It's a small authentic German sausage festival that draws in a lot of people. A lot of out-of-towners come. There's a small carousel set up and there are a few other rides like a Ferris wheel. There are some just for little kids. Like I said, folks come from all over Texas, Arkansas, Oklahoma, and Louisiana for a taste of the authentic German food and beer fest. Folks get dressed up. Some people get really into it," Griff said.

"Have you?" she asked.

His brow shot up.

"What? Dress up?" he asked.

"I think you just answered my question," she said with a laugh.

"Not even when I was a kid," he said with amusement. There was something very appealing about Griff Quinn. The word that came to mind was charming, but it wasn't quite adequate to describe him.

"Don't tell me that you didn't even dress up for trick or treating," she said.

"Not since I was eight years old," he said. "How about you? Do you have any desire to dress up in German clothing?"

Laurel laughed.

"I wouldn't even know what that looked like except the cliché of what is presented on a beer bottle," she said.

"Yeah? I think they pretty much nailed it on all those ales and steins," Griff said on a laugh. The deep rumble that came from his chest only made him sexier.

"There," she pointed, "I think I see the Ferris wheel you mentioned."

One of the beauties of living in this area of Texas was the wide-open skies and the flat land, that made her feel like she could see forever on a clear day. Also, she noted the traffic had increased considerably in the past couple of minutes.

"We are definitely getting close," he said. "The festival opened half an hour ago. Usually, the line comes before the opening. I thought we would be fine swooping in after the gates had been open for a little while."

"If it's this bad now, I can only imagine what it must've looked like an hour ago," she said.

"You'd be surprised the lengths folks go to in order to be first in line. I've been out here for days, watching over the ones who get here early and camp out. It's been dry, so fires can be an issue and we have to nip those in the bud," he said. "Folks are well-meaning, most of the time, but things can get out of hand with tailgating parties when alcohol is involved."

Being here in line would give her more time to get to know the sheriff at least.

"When did you know you wanted to go into law enforcement or become a sheriff?" she asked, wanting to know more about the man sitting in the seat next to her. When she really thought about the fact that she was in a vehicle with a virtual stranger, she surprised herself. Looking back, she had never felt this level of comfort and safety with Timothy. And now that she really thought about it, there had always been a slightly dangerous edge to him that she now realized wasn't as exciting as it might have felt at the time. If she'd known where that dangerous edge would have led, she would have said, *No, thank you.*

No use going down that unproductive road again.

"I grew up around a father who was a sheriff, and didn't know that it was in my blood until I was in high school and had been goofing around like sometimes high schoolers do, testing the boundaries. My father thought it might be a good idea to go out with one of his deputies. Looking back, it was probably more of a babysitting assignment than anything else; Deputy Shaw wasn't more than ten years older than me at the time, barely out of his rookie year. I went to school with the youngest Shaw brother. We knew each other, played on the same sports team. And then we were on this small road, FM 226..."

He paused for a couple of beats as they inched forward toward the festival.

"I know the road you're talking about. It's not far

from here at all. In fact, I take it when I'm going to work sometimes if I want to go a more scenic route," she said.

"Exactly, yes, that's the one. It was on an afternoon shift, broad daylight on a sunny day in the spring. We'd had a lot of rain recently and Deputy Shaw and I were shooting the breeze about the weather. I can admit that I was probably hard to talk to, because I was sulking about the fact that I had to be out there, when I wanted to be with all my buddies who were on a weekend fishing trip, probably popping open a couple at that exact moment," he said.

"I can't imagine a kid who would want to visit his dad's work rather than go out with his buddies," she said. "How old were you?"

"I was probably fifteen or sixteen at the time," he hesitated as they inched forward a little more. "Actually, now that I think about it, I was sixteen because I drove myself to my dad's office."

"What happened?" she asked, fearing the direction this was heading.

"We were on what should have been a routine traffic stop. There was this vehicle driving over the speed limit, kicking up dust." He took another beat of silence. They inched closer to the parking lot that she could actually see at this point. "Officer Shaw got out, like he'd done dozens of times that same week. I can't remember the last thing he said to me. Some kind of joke." He shook his head like he was trying to shake off the bad memory. "Shaw walked up to the vehicle with his hand resting on the butt of his gun like I'd seen him do in the times I'd ridden with him in the past. The vehicle was a lime green Dodge Charger."

"The muscle car," she said when he paused again.

"Yes, that's right. It stuck out in my mind because of the bright color. I also remember it had some kind of dragon design on the trunk. I just remember Deputy Shaw, whose wife was six months pregnant, and how young he was. He had his whole life in front of him as he walked up to the driver's side. Then, the second he turns toward the driver, the blast happened. Time slowed down after that. I'd looked away onto the field and was thinking in that moment how angry I was that I was stuck here on a traffic stop, instead of partying with my buddies. That shotgun blast sent me into what could only be described as shock," he stated.

"You were so young," she said, her heart aching for what he'd gone through.

"I saw the flash out of the corner of my eye, and then I saw Deputy Shaw take a couple of steps back after being shot at point-blank range. There was this stunned look on his face that is stamped into my memory. He couldn't believe what had just happened any more than I could," Griff continued. "The driver of the vehicle just floored it. He kicked up so much dust it was like being caught inside a tornado with weather coming at you from all sides. The dust storm made it next to impossible to see Deputy Shaw."

The truck moved forward, more like a steady crawl at this point as the Ferris wheel grew larger through the front window.

"And then I grabbed his shotgun."

CHAPTER SIX

Griff remembered what happened next like it happened yesterday. "Fitted into the SUV was a rack for Shaw's shotgun. It was a custom job built underneath the bench seat perfectly made. I knew it was there because I'd seen him grab it. So, I took it and by the time I got to Deputy Shaw, he was just sitting there," he said before shaking his head. "I won't go into the details but it was the worst thing I'd ever witnessed."

"I'm so sorry you had to see that," she said, and meant every word. "I can only imagine how traumatic that must have been for a teenager. No one should have to see something like that."

"No, they shouldn't. But, in that moment, I knew being out on the lake partying and being stupid wasn't what I was going to do the rest of my life. In that instant, I realized I would follow in my father's foot-steps and get justice for Deputy Shaw, his wife and kid, and for the younger brother of his that I'd been on the same sports teams with since I could remember," he continued.

"Oh, Griff. I can't even imagine what had to have been going through your mind back then, and yet you were able to turn it around and into your life's work," she said. Those words acted like balm to a wounded soul. Had he really ever healed from the experience? Could anyone? Going through something like that, at any age, changed a person.

"Thank you," he said.

"I mean it. Going through something so traumatic would bring most to their knees. Your strength amazes me," she said.

This wasn't a story he told to many people. In fact, the number would fit on one hand. There was something about the sincerity in her words that soothed the place deep inside him. She seemed to understand his pain on a soul-deep level, and his suspicions about trauma in her past were confirmed.

"Means a lot," he said, clearing the emotion knotting in his throat. A large part of the reason Griff didn't tell people about that story in his past was because even hearing the words again caused him to relive it on some level. The experience gave him purpose. For that, he would be forever grateful. But there was nothing about losing Deputy Shaw that made the lesson worth it.

In senseless times, he'd learned to find something to hang onto in the situation, some thread that kept his sanity intact and his anger from exploding. In this case, he'd sworn to do right by Deputy Shaw's widow, and had delivered on that promise and then some.

"What happened to her?" Laurel asked and he could tell that she was trying to process the details of what had happened and possibly connect the dots as to aspects of his personality today.

"Mrs. Shaw?" he asked. "She lost the baby. Some folks say it was due to grief. I wouldn't argue that point. The baby was born three months premature and there wasn't much doctors could do to save the child, even though specialists were flown in from Dallas and Houston. And then, Cynthia Shaw had a real rough go of it for several years after losing a baby and her husband. But then, she slowly started picking up the pieces of her life. By the time I was twenty, she started dating a baker. Said she wouldn't have to worry about whether or not he came home from the bakery. His schedule was predictable, his job was as safe as it could be, and he was a good person inside and out. They had a family together."

He skipped over the part about sending her money every month out of his own savings until she'd married the baker.

Laurel sat there in silence, hands clasped in her lap for several minutes as they approached the parking lot.

"You helped her out, didn't you?" she asked, when she finally spoke.

"I checked in on her. I needed to know that she ended up okay," he admitted.

"I can tell that you did a whole lot more than that," she began. "But you don't have to share the details with me." She paused for a few beats. "It's enough for me to know you're an incredible human being. Not many

sixteen-year-olds have walked out of that kind of experience and turned it into their life's work. You took a job
that gives justice to people. Very few would have even
visited the widow, let alone support her emotionally
and, I'm guessing, financially. But I think you're too
humble to talk about it."

"Believe it or not, as much as I appreciate what
you're saying, I didn't do all those things to impress
other people, and I especially didn't do it for bragging
rights," he stated. He'd done everything under the radar.
The money came in the form of cash, so the bank
cashiers wouldn't see Cynthia bringing in a check from
him to deposit. The way he saw it, helping out financially was the least he could do.

Did he feel a sense of guilt over witnessing Deputy
Shaw's death? There was no denying it had stuck with
him over the years.

"I know," she said, nodding her head. "I feel like I
maybe learned this lesson a little bit later than most,
but I judge a person's character by their actions and not
their words. It's a trap that I believe a lot of honest
people fall into. Or maybe I just want to believe I'm not
the only one who didn't. Your actions tell me everything
that I need to know about whether or not you're a good
person. And in my book, someone who goes out of their
way for years to help another person is practically a
saint."

Griff shook his head and stomped his brakes as the
truck in front of him made a quick stop.

"That's a lesson we all seem to have to learn the hard
way," Griff said. Based on what Laurel had just said,
there was definitely someone in her life, her past, who'd

not just hurt her but put that fear in her eyes. Griff's fingers tightened around the steering wheel because his thoughts snapped to someone she was close to, someone she was in a relationship with. Nine times out of ten, it was the person closest to a woman who assaulted her. It was awful and made him want to put his fist through a wall that someone who was supposed to love and protect another person would be their biggest threat.

Again, his experience had taught him just how cruel humans could be to one another. It was also the reason he made a very strong effort to get out into the community and participate in things like this festival, not just as a law enforcement officer, but as a human being. It was very important to Griff to get to see and connect with the reason he put his life on the line, and that was to protect the good people out there. To be reminded who they were, see their faces enjoying what they loved to do most.

It would be far too easy to get caught up with the small percentage of bad people out there preying on good folks, and start thinking that was normal. He imagined it was not unlike a soldier, if he or she let themselves stay away too long from what they were serving and protecting. They could lose focus and start believing everyone is bad and everyone is out to hurt others. It was also the reason he'd been close with his cousins. His uncle might have been a bona fide jerk for most of his life, but that had caused him and his brothers to circle the wagons and look out for each other more. They didn't exactly have a parent figure to rely on.

"Let me know if you spot a good parking space," he said, changing the subject. Considering Laurel's mood had intensified, he wanted to find a lighter topic. Their conversation had gone down a different path and he wanted to see her smile again instead of frown. The few times he'd seen her really smile, the way she lit up, caused him to smile in return. Something told him, probably a combination of hard-won experience combined with instinct, this beautiful person didn't laugh nearly enough. He wanted to change that fact and see her eyes light up again, even if it was only for a few seconds.

"There's a spot," she said pointing to the next aisle over.

The parking lot filled with vehicles reminded him of an ant farm.

"If I can get over there, it's ours," he said as he navigated around a car with its flashers on, indicating it had found a spot.

Griff passed two more vehicles, narrowly missing the sideview mirror of an SUV. Laurel's revelation sat heavy on his chest and in his heart. The implication behind it explained the haunted look in her eyes.

By the time Griff made it around to the parking spot, a zippy little Nissan Rogue beat him to it.

"Over there," she said, pointing to another one.

"We'll give it a whirl," he said, feeling like a mouse stuck in a maze, trying to be the first to the cheese.

At this point, his hopes of being first to a spot had dimmed considerably. His point was proved when a BMW came from seemingly nowhere to grab the spot first. Griff was unfazed.

"I'm surprised the traffic is so heavy this long after the opening. They usually let cars in an hour before the gates open to alleviate some of this," he said. "We might have been better off parking in the field and walking."

"We can always double back," she offered.

"It might be faster than this," he stated.

"To the field it is," she said with a small smile. It was an improvement, and he'd take it. Plus, this would give them a little more time in the truck to talk.

"What about you, by the way?" he asked. "Any siblings?"

"No. I was brought up by my grandmother," she said. "I might have half-siblings out there somewhere, but I have no idea if they exist and who they are if they do."

He nodded, and then waited. Peppering her with questions would put her on the defensive. In Griff's experience, silence was sometimes the best way to get someone to start talking.

A few seconds ticked by. Then, a few more as he navigated toward the exit.

"I secretly always wished for a big family," she said. "I've never told anyone that and I'm not sure why I'm saying it to you. But, I always wanted sisters and brothers."

"Coming from a large family, I can tell you there are pluses and minuses," he said.

"Mostly pluses, right?"

"In my case, yes," he admitted.

"There would always be someone around to play with," she continued, and there was a whole lot more animation in her voice and on her facial expression now.

She lit up like a string of lights during the holiday season.

"True enough," he agreed.

"And help around the house," she said.

"Or in my case, helping around the ranch," he stated.

"That must have been wonderful," she said.

"There were certainly wonderful times."

"With all those people around, there must not have been any—"

"Privacy," he interjected.

"Oh." Her forehead wrinkled. "I was going to say loneliness. But, I'm sure both are true."

Griff felt his muscles tense at the revelation. No one deserved to be lonely in life, least of all someone as thoughtful and kind as Laurel.

"You know, I've been in a room full of people before and still felt lonely. Funny how that works," he said.

"When I really think about it, that's true," she said after a thoughtful pause. "I think I fell into the trap of the grass being greener on the other side."

"I wouldn't trade the way I grew up for anything," he said, wishing she could have experienced the same thing. "There were definitely some downsides, as I'm sure there are in every family. But I always had a friend around and couldn't be closer with my cousins and brothers. Despite my father and uncle doing nothing but fighting their entire lives, their attitude didn't trickle down to us. Maybe because we grew up watching two brothers take opposite sides just for the sake of it. Seeing what that did to their relationships, or should I say non-relationship, caused us to follow a different blueprint."

"In my fantasy, everyone got along in a big family. Pretty *Sound of Music* when I really think about it," she said.

He glanced over in time to see that red blush crawl to her cheeks again.

"Well, I grew up with a whole lot of young boys, teenage boys, and there was a lot of teasing and barn fights where we had to find a substitute for snowballs, if you know what I mean," he said with a chuckle.

"Horse manure?"

"You can throw it far if it's dry," he said. "Besides, we always had on gloves when we were working in the barn, so it wasn't as gross to pick it up as one might think. Looking back, when it's put like that, we were hellions. I'm not sure how anyone put up with us."

"Did you grow up at the ranch?" she asked. The amusement in her voice said she enjoyed the barn story, much to his relief.

"I did, and I spent a whole lot of time in the barn, especially when things got rough at home. Being sheriff comes with a lot of stress and there's a reason the divorce rate is so high among law enforcement officers," he said.

"The stress must be unimaginable at times," she stated, but there was a cold undertone to her voice that made him believe she'd had a not-so-great run-in with someone who was sworn to uphold the law.

Griff didn't know much about the mystery woman in his passenger seat. He counted himself a decent judge of character and all the feedback about her in town corroborated his belief. His mind snapped to her possibly having dated someone on the job and having a bad experience. And yet, wouldn't she be more afraid of him than she seemed to be if that was true?

"I see you weren't the only one with this brilliant idea," she said, nodding toward the pair of trucks already parked.

"Now you know these people are seasoned festival goers," he said as he parked. He hopped out quickly to open her door, not because she couldn't do it for herself but because he lived by a code that said he was a gentleman. Chivalry was not dead. It was up to whoever sat in the passenger seat to accept or decline the gesture.

———

Laurel allowed Griff to open the passenger door for her, thinking it was a nice change of pace from the last person she'd dated. She glanced around wearily, looking for anyone who ducked behind a car quickly as her gaze swept the area. She'd had a short break in recent months from this level of paranoia, but the day's events were catching up to her and had triggered her alert system.

No matter how much she tried to shake off the feeling, she had the sensation of fire ants walking across her skin. The main thing holding her together was Griff's steady hand that she took as she exited the truck. He closed the door and locked the vehicle behind them.

Laurel walked so close to Griff, they were literally arm-to-arm and bumping against each other with each step. He reached for her hand the moment she reached for his, and they linked their fingers after contact. And boy, what contact that was. Being skin-to-skin brought a ripple of awareness up her arm and through her body, spreading warmth through her. She had that tingly feeling as she tried to adjust to being so close to Griff's strong, male presence—a presence that could fill a room. Thankfully, they were outdoors where some of the heat and chemistry pinging between them could dissipate.

She brought her other hand up across her body to hold onto his forearm.

There was a sea of Stetsons, cowgirl boots, and denim. There was something calming and relaxing about it all and the feel of being back in Texas. It felt good to be outside again, no matter how much her fear response wanted to make her turn tail and run.

She was determined to go out in public again. It had been nine long months that she'd been hiding from everyone and everything. And then two years before that, she'd been watching every step, careful not to go into public any more than she had to, including going into the grocery store. She'd even had to start getting nearly all of her household supplies delivered in order to avoid running into any one of Timothy's old friends, or the guys he hung out with, or worse yet, his parents.

Not that they would be inside a grocery store doing their own shopping, but they would be at the mall or one of the popular restaurants in the area. Laurel had become the queen of takeout on the days she didn't have it in her to cook for herself. Marissa and her family had been amazing. But the rest of town had been against her and very firmly on Timothy's side.

There was something freeing about being in this crowd where no one knew her or anything about her past, and especially about the horrific trauma that always seemed to be one step behind her.

Here, no one looked at her with disgust or anger. Here, she could just blend right into the crowd. There was something beautiful about that.

As they neared the ticket booth, Griff turned to her and asked, "Since I invited you to come with me today, I'd like to pay for your ticket inside. But I wanted to check with you first, and make sure you are okay with that."

"Sure," she said. "It doesn't offend me in the least." In fact, she appreciated him even more for asking, and not just assuming he had to cover all of her expenses. Then again, there was something incredibly special about Griff, that she realized were the kinds of qualities that didn't come around in a person often in one lifetime. He was the total package and a piece of her wished she could stick around Gunner and continue to get to know him.

The dark clouds would close in soon, though. She was already jumpy and fearful, which usually meant it was time to move on from a place. The shadow sighting this morning might have been a signal she was getting too comfortable here.

And as much as she wanted to plant roots somewhere, she knew better than to let her guard down for long. In St. Louis, the first city she'd tried to get lost in on her way to Texas, it had only taken a week for Timothy's best friend to appear at the diner where she'd taken a job as a hostess. Thankfully, she'd come in through the back door and heard his voice right away.

Her exit from the building had been swift, and she'd gone undetected. He'd made the reason for his stop clear when she'd overheard him asking if someone by her description worked there and, if so, when her next shift was.

Another stroke of luck had come when Roseanne, the hostess who was on duty at the time, had said the schedule hadn't come out yet but that Laurel wasn't due in that day. She could kiss Roseanne for covering.

Laurel hadn't waited around to hear James' response. She'd bolted through the kitchen, hopped into the car she'd rented, and headed west to throw him off her trail. She'd racked her brain trying to figure out how he'd found her. Then, her mistake had glared at her when she stopped to fill up the tank. She'd kept one credit card that had been from an account she was authorized to use from her grandmother. Thinking it would be safe to use since it wasn't technically in her name, she'd purchased gas with it.

Clearly, she'd thought wrong, and James Whitney had found her. Timothy had the kinds of friends who vowed to take care of each other. The fact they'd seemed willing to go through thick and thin together had drawn her toward Timothy initially. Of course, she'd had no idea the bond was less like brothers and more like gang members. There had been a bond thicker than blood between them.

Now? She realized just how far they would go for revenge. Being on the flip side of the coin, she got a bird's eye view of the wrath that came with hurting one of their own. She was an outsider, an outcast, and someone to be 'handled' or 'taken care of.'

Laurel felt a pair of eyes boring holes through her from somewhere behind as a familiar cold chill raced down her back.

CHAPTER SEVEN

Griff felt the instant Laurel's muscles tensed as they approached the ticket counter and the crowd around them thickened. He turned his head to the side, toward her, and whispered, "Everything all right?"

"I have this bad feeling someone is watching me," she said.

"Which direction?" he asked, keeping his voice barely above a whisper.

"From behind, but please don't look right now. It's probably just me," she said.

"Being with me might draw attention to you," he said by way of apology.

"Two tickets, Sheriff?" Rachel asked from behind the plexiglass. There was a metal speaker around where Rachel's mouth was, and a slot underneath the glass to exchange credit cards and a receipt much like the one at the pharmacy drive-through.

"Yes, ma'am," he stated, releasing Laurel's hand in

order to fish his wallet out of his back pocket. He located his credit card and then slipped it inside the metal divot.

Rachel took the card, swiped it, and then tapped the computer screen a few times before a pair of tickets printed out on his side. Next, the credit card, along with a receipt, was returned underneath the glass.

Griff took the tickets and returned his credit card to his wallet. As he tucked it inside his back pocket, he risked a glance backward. A quick scan of the faces behind them didn't reveal anyone particularly focused on Laurel. A couple of folks had already said hello while the two of them walked toward the bay of ticket counters, especially as the crowd thickened.

There were more than a few surprised faces, considering it looked like he was on a date. Griff usually got attention when he went out, and a couple of his dates had complained about other women being rude to them in the bathroom, and he'd even witnessed a waitress or two giving his dates the cold shoulder. Griff wasn't the type to parade a new person around in front of someone from his past. In a small town like Gunner, it was impossible to keep them separate all the time. Which was also the reason he preferred to have first dates out at the lake on a picnic or an informal barbecue at home.

Like it or not, his social life was news, and he was reminded of the fact as more folks stared at him and Laurel. As he walked past the counter and toward the gate, he realized that he had probably had one of the more recognizable faces in Gunner.

Instinct had him reaching for Laurel's hand, clasping their fingers together. Holding hers felt like the most natural thing. He took note of how much she was glued to his side. Not that he minded it one bit. He didn't. In fact, having this close contact with Laurel awakened feelings that had been buried deep.

The reason that she was so close to him caused anger to rise up. Her body slightly trembled and he knew without a doubt there'd been some trauma in her past, and he would bet money on it being recent. Getting her to open up and talk about it was a whole other issue. She'd already put out some hints there'd been trouble. Just how deep and how much was of concern at this point.

At this point, his law enforcement instincts had kicked into high alert. For her safety's sake, he wanted to know what she was running from. Besides, he was great at his job and if there was some way he could help her, he wouldn't hesitate. There was something else he knew about people in all his years of dealing with them. It was impossible to help someone until they were ready to help themselves.

They walked through the space between the ticket counter and the gate with throngs of folks. When they approached the person taking tickets, right before it was their turn, Deputy Rustler greeted them.

"Hey, boss," Deputy Rustler said, his gaze momentarily bounced from Laurel and then back to Griff. A split second of surprise flashed behind his eyes until he reined it back in.

"Deputy Rustler, this is my friend Laurel." Griff purposely didn't mention her last name. At this point, he wasn't one hundred percent sure the last name folks knew her by was real. He wasn't concerned about her being in WitSec. The fear that she had seemed to indicate she was all on her own. He'd be surprised if she had any protection at all other than a sharp radar.

His curiosity about the mystery woman was growing. His need for answers was starting to create a physical ache in his chest. His desire to protect her was a force of its own.

So, yes, when he took her home later, he was going to ask her politely if she would be willing to open up about what she was running from. Or whom, he should say. And if she didn't, he would keep an extra eye on the cabin. Not because he needed to stalk her, but because he wanted to watch out for any suspicious characters lurking around.

He remembered the empty bathroom cabinets and the suitcase that had been sitting on top of her bed. It was probably time to face the reality that he had maybe a couple more hours with her, and then she very well might disappear from his life forever.

"Really nice to meet you," Deputy Rustler said.

Laurel smiled even though it didn't spark in her eyes. It was perfunctory and yet he appreciated the effort nonetheless.

"You too, Deputy," she said.

Griff felt her torso press a little more into his side. Her grip on his hand intensified. Pretty much everything about her body language said *Get me out of here*.

"Normally, this is where I check people's bags and wave the magic wand to see if anyone is trying to bring any contraband inside," Deputy Rustler said. "Clearly, since you are the sheriff, I trust that you are good to go.

Rustler took a dramatic sidestep and then waved his

hand like he was presenting the gate. Griff recognized that his deputy was trying to lighten Laurel's mood. Lots of women had a difficult time dating law enforcement, given the dangers of the job. Most went into it with apprehension, so they tried to roll out the red carpet for each other.

Griff appreciated the extra effort.

"Thank you very much," Griff said. "Don't mind if we do."

If Laurel's fingers tightened around Griff's hand anymore, there would be complete blood loss to his fingers.

Griff took a couple of steps toward the turnstile and then paused with the line as it slowed since folks had to go through individually. Again, he tilted his head toward Laurel's ear, trying to ignore the scent of fresh flowers and the temptation to bring his lips down on hers as she looked up at him. He'd thought about the brief kiss they'd shared more times than he wanted to in the past couple of hours. Their lips had barely touched, and yet there'd been more sizzle and promise in those few seconds than in any of the kisses in his past, bar none. That was saying something considering he'd been dating for well over a decade at this point.

"Are you sure you want to go inside?" he asked before hitting the turnstile.

She blinked a couple of times and it looked like she was seriously considering her options for a few long seconds. The line moved and it was their turn to walk inside.

And then her chin jutted out, her shoulders went

back, and a sense of pride and indignation seemed to fill her.

"I haven't been out in a public place in a very long time," she said. "I'm not going to lie and say anything about this is easy for me right now. There are things from my past...but I really want to go to this festival with you today."

She tilted her head and looked up at him, capturing his gaze. His heart skipped a few beats.

"And I am determined not to let my imagination get the best of me, or my fears stop me from having fun," she said.

"That's all I need to hear," he said. And then he felt her fingers relax just a little.

Griff was even more determined to show Laurel a good time. She deserved it and he wanted to be the one to give it to her. Besides, this might be his only shot to take her out or show her how to relax again. Even if it was only for a few hours.

"What would you like to do first?" he asked, stopping off at the ticket machine since the festival was cashless.

Laurel glanced around, wide-eyed. The crowd had eased now that they'd gotten away from the gates. "Well, I already smell the pretzels so that's a guaranteed stop at some point," she said with just enough spark in her eyes to egg him on. "And there is the Ferris wheel."

"Wouldn't be a trip to the festival without either of those," he said, getting into the spirit of the moment. It was funny how someone's mood could change with the right surroundings.

"Exactly," she said. "There's so much food and it all smells amazing."

"How hungry are you?" he asked.

"I could seriously eat," she said, without skipping a beat.

He checked his watch and it was already half past four. Not too early for a heavy snack.

"How about a sausage link and a beer?" he asked.

"Yes. I'm surprised you didn't hear my stomach growling in line. Both of those sound like heaven," she said.

"Let this evening get started." Griff led them through the throngs of people, at one point feeling like salmon swimming upstream, as he led them to his favorite sausage link vendor. "You know, everybody comes to the festival for the sausage links but what they don't realize is that it's all about the sauerkraut."

"Oh, really?" she asked.

"Just remember that I'm the one who told you so, when you taste what I have in store," he said. "Sauerkraut. It's the most underrated side dish, and yet it packs the most flavor. I would go so far as to say sausage would be nothing without it."

"Come to think of it, sausage does taste a whole lot better when it has sauerkraut next to it," she agreed.

"See," he said.

"I might have been late, but I got there," she quipped and seemed to be enjoying the banter as much as he was. She was bright and had a funny side that he would like to have the opportunity to get to know a whole lot better. In this case, time was most definitely not on his side.

Jeb's line was much shorter than the one they'd waited in, trying to get inside the festival. The minute Jeb made eye contact with Griff, his friend started waving them over. Filling a couple of baskets, he then instructed the employee at the tap to pour two steins.

Griff tried to get his friend's attention to get him to walk over to the cash register. Jeb just made a face and then waved Griff off. At some point, the man was going to have to let Griff pay his way.

One of the workers waved Griff over to the fresh baskets. There was a little table behind the booth for when Jeb or one of his workers took a break. About twenty feet away, there was an open courtyard with a few trees for shade and a smattering of picnic tables.

Jeb always insisted Griff eat at the small picnic table positioned behind the booth and tonight was no exception. The booth was hopping and getting Jeb's attention for longer than two seconds was going to be a problem. The man held up a finger, ducked below the counter to rummage in a box below, and came up with a blue checkered tablecloth. Somehow, he managed to produce a little vase and a single white flower. A daisy?

After handing off the items, one of the workers set up the table in the back. The picnic table was also sheltered by a tree, blocking the intense sun that made it feel a whole lot more like late summer than fall.

"Looks like we have special seating," Griff said, walking Laurel to the area behind the booth that was set up to look like a proper table at a restaurant.

"I feel so special," Laurel said with a look of appreciation. "This is a real-life *Lady and the Tramp* moment."

Griff laughed and then pretended to be offended at the reference to him being a flea-bitten stray.

"I'll have you know that I have my own collar," he said on a laugh, trying to remember the storyline, despite it running multiple times in his office. He'd put that movie on inside his office on repeat when there was a small child around who needed to be there with parents. *Lady and the Tramp* was one he didn't mind hearing over and over again. Besides, it seemed to be a real crowd pleaser with the ten and under set. It was one of those timeless cartoons that all kids seemed to enjoy, whether he was offering a distraction for a little girl or a little boy.

"Good to know," she said with a smile.

Sitting here underneath the shade tree with Laurel felt like one of the most intimate moments of his life. It was as though they were in a bubble, while a whole lot of activity happened around them. Nothing could get through. Nothing could distract them from each other. Nothing could pull attention away from this moment happening between them.

In that moment, he decided he hadn't watched *Lady and the Tramp* nearly enough.

———

"When you're right, you're right," Laurel said to Griff after taking a bite of sausage with the sauerkraut. She washed the bite down with a sip of beer and a little mewl of pleasure escaped. This was quite possibly the best combination of German fare she'd ever tasted.

She took another sip of beer from the silver stein,

and of course, it was the perfect taste to wash down the perfect bite.

"You better watch out, if word gets out about this sausage and sauerkraut situation, the line we were in for parking will be nothing in comparison to the one that will assemble for this booth," she said.

Griff slowly brought his index fingers to his lips as though shushing her.

"That's why I don't talk about it with anyone else," he said with a conspiratorial grin. "They do plenty of business over these three days to finance half their year. I keep a couple of secrets close to my chest and this is one of them."

She felt the blood leave her face at the thought of Griff holding secrets. It meant nothing, she reminded herself. He was talking about keeping a favorite food quiet, not something serious like what he really did for a living. The differences between him and Timothy were huge.

"I can totally see why," she said, regaining her footing in the conversation. "Nothing ruins a place faster than good press."

They both chuckled and the mood improved. Laurel felt like she'd already been on a rollercoaster all day. Built on emotions, hers had run the gamut. And yet being out here—as scary as that might be—felt so much better than hiding. There'd been times, especially recently, when she had had the thought that if she had to hide much longer she might explode.

Hiding was hard.

The only thing harder than hiding was dying. There was no way she would put her life unduly at risk. She could admit that after the whole diner incident, early on, she'd been shell-shocked and probably overly careful to ensure no one could follow her or find her.

Conversation came to a standstill while they ate. That always seemed to happen when folks were hungry and the food was incredible. The power nap she'd taken at home before Griff's arrival was paying off big time, or perhaps it was just being around him that made her want to stay awake and alert. Either way, she forced her shoulders to relax as she took in a slow breath, then polished off her basket of food. Food this good deserved all of her attention.

The beer in the stein, on the other hand, was probably more than she wanted or needed. The few sips she'd taken satisfied her. Plus, there was no way she intended to risk not having a clear head. Even now, even with Griff, even in the presence of a sheriff, she knew better than to let her guard down for long.

Laurel picked up her empty basket and tossed it along with her plastic utensils into the nearby trash can. She placed her stein in a separate bin for wash and reuse. Griff followed suit. After dumping his trash, he linked their fingers.

"The Ferris wheel is best saved for when the sun is going down. It will have the best views, and you feel like you can see forever," he said.

She tried to ignore the fact he seemed to know a whole lot about the most romantic time in which to ride the ride, or the fact that she'd taken plenty of side-eye from the late twenties, early thirties single ladies as they walked past while holding hands. She got it. Griff Quinn was clearly considered a catch in Gunner. Then again, a man this gorgeous would be considered a catch in all the major cities too. Add his personality into the mix and the fact his last name associated him with money, and she was certain the gold diggers would climb out of the woodwork for a chance with the handsome sheriff.

As they walked back into the stream of folks, her muscles chorded. She could do this, despite the fact it seemed strange to be out among groups of people after being isolated for so long. She could only hope the feeling of discomfort would dissipate soon, as she got the hang of being in public again. Despite being more of an introvert, she actually enjoyed concerts and going into crowded buildings like popular art galleries. She missed going to a coffee shop with her laptop and just hanging out, like she'd done while putting herself through school.

And, probably most of all, she missed companionship. There was something special about having a person who cared about your day and how you felt. Her grandmother had been the last person she could say truly cared. Timothy had put up a good front, attentive in the early days of their relationship. There'd been signs, of course, but the blinders she'd been wearing had kept her from homing in on those. Hindsight, she thought as she tried to shake the memories.

When Griff tugged her closer, her stomach performed a summersault routine.

"Hey," he said. "Everything okay?"

"Yes, all good," she said. When she glanced up and made eye contact, it was obvious he'd been picking up on her mood shift. "Maybe not right this second, but it will be."

The reassurance seemed to resonate as he nodded and exhaled a little. "I'm here if you want to ditch this place and talk. We could sit in the truck for privacy," he said as a few folks waved at him. Every few steps someone nodded and smiled or a kid waved.

"Now I know what it's like to be seen with a celebrity," she teased, purposely not answering his question while motioning toward a little girl with pigtails and braces who was beaming at the sheriff.

"How's your kitten, Suzanne?" he asked, bending down to look the girl in the eye.

Suzanne's reactions to the sheriff were a mix of excitement and calm. The two were an odd pairing, to be sure, but he seemed to have the same effect on everyone around him.

"Mr. Mittens is all better. My mom says it's thanks to you," Suzanne said. She practically threw her spindly arms around his neck, knocking him off balance to the point he had to put his hand down to stop from being bowled over. Laurel was struck by how safe the little girl seemed with the sheriff and how ridiculously adorable he was being with her.

This kid made Laurel smile. She had once believed she would have kids at some point. The past three years had convinced her to think twice about making a life-time commitment. Losing her grandmother had upended Laurel's emotions. She didn't want to blame her lapse in judgment about Timothy on being blinded by losing the only family she'd known. And yet, she couldn't ignore the timing.

"I didn't do anything you wouldn't do when you grow a little bigger," Griff said to Suzanne.

His comment elicited an ear-to-ear smile from the young girl.

Did he have to be so perfect?

Right man. Wrong time.

So much of life, she'd learned, was about timing.

CHAPTER EIGHT

Griff untangled himself from Suzanne's little arms as politely as he could. Her mother walked over and put a hand on the little girl's shoulder with a warm smile.

"Come on, sweetie," Carla Jenson said. Her gaze bounced from Griff to Laurel and back. Her eyebrow raised slightly, and she smiled awkwardly. "Let the sheriff have fun on his day off."

"Be good for your mom. Okay, kiddo?" he said to Suzanne as he pushed off his knees to stand up. The little girl beamed up at him.

"Yes, sir," Suzanne said with a salute, before her mother tugged her daughter away in the opposite direction with the promise of cotton candy.

"I didn't know cotton candy was German fare," Laurel said with a look. "But that kid was adorable. She actually made me think I might want one someday."

"I'm pretty sure that was the slickest move on her mother's part. Also, it is a festival," Griff said with a shrug as he let the last part of her comment roll right

off him. Or at least he tried. The sudden and unex-
pected image of Laurel holding their child in her arms
assaulted him. This was normally the point where he
started seeing what he didn't like in the other person
and why they weren't 'the one.'

"Well, it's not hard to spot the people who work
here," she pointed out, breaking into his thoughts.

"Or the people who are really into it." Griff motioned
toward a family with five kids ranging in age from a six-
month-old in its mother's arms, to a pre-pubescent tween.
The entire family was dressed in matching outfits. "Those
knee-length pants are called lederhosen." Three of the
boys were dressed alike with their father. The girl's were
identical to the mother. "And she is wearing a dirndl."

"They're adorable or completely weird. I can't
decide," Laurel said with a laugh, and it was the most
musical thing to his ears.

"Those terms don't have to be mutually exclusive,"
he said, and couldn't help but smile back. She had that
effect on him. To be honest, it was refreshing that
someone could affect him for a change. Every date he'd
been on in the past couple of years had been like
drinking the same tepid cup of coffee over and over
again ad nauseum.

"True enough," she agreed.

They both chuckled.

"Actually, why do you not own a pair of those,"
Laurel said on another laugh.

"Not happening. Ever," he shot back.

He reached for her fingers and she immediately
clasped her hands around his. Contact caused another

jolt of electricity to shoot through him, the intensity of which he thought he might never get used to.

"I can take you over to the folk dancing tent next," he offered.

Laurel balked. "I think I'll take a pass on that one, unless it's spectator only," she said.

"They actually expect you to join in," he said. He snapped the fingers on his left hand like he was just as disappointed. In truth, he had no intention of getting out on that dance floor unless she dragged him. The offer was for her and her alone. Besides, most of the women he'd dated complained about him not taking them dancing nearly enough.

"Maybe next time," she said, and then seemed to catch herself. Both seemed to realize this was their only shot at a date.

The thought caused an ache to well up in his chest that caught him off guard. There were so many secrets with Laurel. Although, he'd narrowed the possibilities down, he wished he knew specifically what was going to cause her to bolt. Would she even be in the cabin by morning?

Griff decided not to focus on what he didn't know and couldn't change. He had this moment, right now, with her and that was going to have to be enough.

"How about games?" she asked, and her eyes lit up at the possibility and his traitorous heart gave a flip. So much for playing it cool and keeping his feelings in check around Laurel.

"Games it is," he said, before walking her over to the small midway. "Pick your pleasure."

"Hmmmm," she said, like she was seriously considering her options.

"You can throw a softball and try to knock all the steins off the small round table," he said.

"I always thought that game was a racket. Have you ever seen anyone win?" she asked.

"Back in the day, I might have been able to do it." He rolled his right shoulder a couple of times like he was warming up to pitch. "It's all about finding the right spot to knock the steins off. You have to make a clean hit and at the right speed or you'll end up with a spinner."

"Sounds like you know what you're doing," she said. "Want to give it a try?"

"No promises," he said.

"This date has already exceeded all my expectations," she said and then seemed to catch herself a second time. "I mean, this is probably not a real date, like, you are just being kind to the new person in town and—"

"I asked you out," he interrupted as gently as he could. "To me, that's a date."

Her shoulders dropped as she released a breath.

"Good," she said, "because all I really meant to say is that I'm having a really good time. And I need to thank you for reminding me what that was like. It's been a really long time since I let my hair down."

Griff had to resist the urge to dive into the loaded meaning of what Laurel had just said. Little by little, information was coming out. If he was patient and had enough time, he realized she would likely tell him everything of her own accord.

Time.

It seemed in short supply when it came to the mystery woman beside him.

"You're welcome. I'm happy to hear you're having a good time. But the night is still young, and I think I can bring my game up a couple of notches," he said. His chest shouldn't puff up at the admission she liked him. That was essentially what she'd just said. He liked her too. A whole lot, actually. "Now, let's see if I can get you one of those koala bears."

"It's bigger than my bed," she teased.

"The higher the risk, the better the reward," he said as they walked over to the game attendant who was standing in the middle of the booth.

"Come on over and see if you can win a prize for the beautiful lady," the attendant said.

"Let me see what I can do," Griff said, before rolling his shoulder a couple more times. He let go of Laurel's hand so he could do a couple of practice throws without the ball.

"How much does ten dollars buy me?" he asked. The games were still cash and carry.

"That will get you three tries. Throw another ten down there and you'll get eight softballs instead. What a deal," the man said. He had on an apron loaded with softballs.

"Appreciate the offer," Griff stated. "I really do. But if I can't get it in three, it's not going to happen today."

"If you change your mind before you throw the first pitch, the deal is on the table. Once you release a ball, the deal is over." The attendant looked to be in his mid-forties with a ruddy complexion and a belly that hung over the apron.

"I'll take my chances." Griff handed over a ten-dollar bill and the attendant immediately tucked the bill inside his apron.

It didn't look like the man had a whole lot of business, because this was probably one of the hardest games in the whole place. This, and the ring toss, had always been his nemesis. However, he used to be able to throw a pretty decent pitch and he was about to put his abilities to the test.

"There's a science to this," he whispered to Laurel. Most people made the mistake of throwing the pitch too hard, like throwing a bowling ball down the lane. That was not going to be Griff's game. Surgical precision in where he struck would get him where he needed to go, because the whole point was to get the other steins to help do the work. Too much force and it threw the steins too far. Too light and he'd miss the platform altogether. This game, like many things in life, required finesse.

He picked up one of the balls and stepped up to the thigh-high barrier. One more glance over at Laurel for inspiration, and he threw a change-up pitch with just enough force to tip the bottom steins over. There were five, stacked three on the bottom, two in the middle, and one top. The ball hit two of the steins on the bottom row; the middle and right stein high. Impact caused the steins to topple over and immediately fall off. The second level pair of steins dropped and hit just at the right angle to spin. Both spun off. The last stein, the one on top, dropped almost as if in slow motion. It spun around long ways and made it to the edge of the platter and then slowed. If someone blew on it, it would literally fall off. All Griff's muscles tensed as Laurel grabbed hold of his forearms. The handle skirted the edge, keeping the stein from toppling off.

Laurel's fingers dug into his skin as a small crowd gathered around them. The single stein teetered on the edge. Griff had the urge to jump up and down just to shake the ground enough for the stein to topple over.

Just when he thought the stein was going to stop, it tipped over the side. The small crowd cheered as the stein fell off. The group erupted in applause and before he realized what was happening, Laurel jumped into his arms. With her body flush against his, all rational thought flew out the window.

Caught up in the moment and unable to resist the draw to the woman in his arms, he dropped his head down and pressed his lips to hers.

More of that electricity jolted through him at multiple points of contact. His body was a virtual battlefield of impulse to the likes of which he'd never experienced from a simple hug and a kiss. Then again, Laurel was not an average person, so he should have expected this. Well, maybe not *this*.

She parted her lips and teased his tongue inside her mouth, where he tasted the remnants of sauerkraut and a hint of beer. The sauerkraut tasted even better this way. Don't even get him started on the beer.

"Your prize," the attendant said, breaking into the moment happening between them.

Griff opened his eyes and locked onto Laurel's. In

that moment, he couldn't help thinking that the real prize was in his arms at that very moment.

———

When the reality that a rather large spotlight was on them sunk in, Laurel wanted to shrink inside herself and disappear. This whole scenario was the exact opposite of keeping a low profile in order to stay out of sight. Being with Griff Quinn, it turned out, was big news and a factor she hadn't considered when he asked her out. In hindsight, she really should have been able to guess one of, if not the, most eligible bachelor in a small town would draw everyone's eye. The huge misstep on her part might just cost more than she bargained for.

But the kiss they'd shared was so far beyond anything she'd ever experienced. In that moment, nothing had mattered except the feel of his lips moving against hers and how incredible his hands felt on her. It had been impossible to think clearly. The only thing she was certain of now was that no others would measure up. Ever. Griff's kisses were the gold standard.

The moment her feet hit the ground, she had to force them to stay rooted when all they wanted to do was run. All eyes were on them, causing her chest to constrict. Griff loosened his grip around her waist as a look of surprise widened his eyes. The knot in Laurel's chest tightened until she could no longer breathe. The air around her thinned and it felt like the entire crowd was staring at her. She reminded herself to take in a couple of deep breaths as she backed away from Griff, shaking her head.

Laurel looked him straight in the eye and said, "This is a mistake. I can't do this."

This whole date was a bad idea. As much as she'd been determined to enjoy this day, she'd failed. Until she was one hundred percent safe, it was too risky to be in such a public place. Going out in the open like this was too scary and dangerous. One of Timothy's buddies could have tracked her down, or potentially would after this. People would talk about her now and word would get out about her being in Gunner. Folks would have questions and wouldn't think twice about a stranger coming to town asking seemingly innocent questions about trying to get back in touch with an old friend, or whatever excuse a stalker might use.

Not enough time had passed since leaving Chicago. Laurel took a couple of steps backward, tripped and landed on top of metal. A piece jabbed her in the backside. She glanced around in time to realize she'd just fallen into a baby stroller. She scrambled back to her feet as panic gripped her, waiting to hear the wail of the baby she no-doubt hurt in the process.

Thankfully, the baby was safe in her mother's arms. The mother, however, was not amused and Laurel couldn't blame the woman for shooting daggers from her eyes.

The horror and embarrassment of what had just happened caused Laurel to jump to her feet and immediately apologize. Sticking around would only bring more attention to her. She mumbled a few more apologies to the crowd as she back peddled. Then, she took off running in the opposite direction, needing to get as far away from the crowd as she could. The thought of the potential for camera phones to be pointed in her direction, or her image ending up in some viral social media message, caused her chest to squeeze.

Somewhere in the background, she heard Griff's voice shouting her name. He sounded stunned and now she was horribly embarrassed to face him. What must he think of her that any little noise or attention had her ready to literally jump out of her skin and bolt? That was the thing about trauma. The journey to feeling whole again was fraught with potholes. She'd just stepped in a big one. Plus, the whole going on a date, thinking she was ready for that step, was clearly so misguided. The whole episode set her back even more.

Right man. Wrong time.

Laurel pushed her legs as fast as she could go, dodging in and out of people until she reached the front gate. The exit was right next to it, a giant turnstile with a worker standing to the right. The lederhosen-ed man had a stamp in his fist and seemed to be asking each individual before they exited whether or not they would be returning. Some probably needed to retrieve a supply from their vehicle, but all she could think about was busting through the line to get on the other side of the metal. She reminded herself to calm down and take a couple of breaths. As it was, her thighs burned, her side cramped, and she was not in the right state of mind to make a decision.

In this moment, she couldn't help but wonder if it would always feel like one of Timothy's buddies or his cop cousin would constantly be one step behind. Her body involuntarily shivered at the thought. Would she ever be free of their threats? Or was this what her life was going to be from now on? Constantly looking over her shoulder; hiding out in location after location, never truly putting down roots; limiting her life to work and no social life?

It had been nine months since she'd spoken to her best friend Marissa. Nine long months since she'd heard her friend's voice or listened to how big the twins were getting, and whether or not they'd mastered sleeping through the night.

The line stopped and Laurel did too, barely a second before crashing into the back of the man in front of her. She desperately wished for a temporary reprieve from her racing thoughts that immediately shifted to Griff.

All she could think was that if he'd liked her before, the ship had most definitely sailed now. At least it would be easy for him to write off this date as a bad experience and move on because she was certain she'd just set a record for how much she'd just made the guy regret kissing her. She'd freaked out moments after the best kiss of her life, but it was probably just as well. A relationship between her and Griff couldn't go anywhere. It had been naïve to think she could stay under the radar on a date with him.

If this line would just hurry up and move, she could get out of here and out his hair for good, she thought as her heart pounded the inside of her ribcage, trying to ignore if that was truly what she wanted.

No. She could be honest about it. Had to be honest about it. The chemistry she felt with him was special and deserved a chance. Dragging him into her drama wasn't exactly the way to start a new relationship, and tangling him up in her problems could put him in just as much danger.

If embarrassment could kill a person, she'd be dead. Life would be so much easier if she could get out of here, get home to finish packing, and then get on the road. She could figure out her next destination once she cleared her mind and got out of town. All she needed was a direction in which to point. West. She decided to head west and just drive until an idea came to her.

She glanced backward, praying Griff hadn't followed her. So, of course, there he was, standing ten feet away from her and leaning up against a light post with his arms crossed. He was staring down at his boots and his chest was barely heaving despite what had been a serious run to keep up with her.

The fact he stayed back, even though she took another few steps forward, said he wasn't trying to stop her from leaving. And then it dawned on her why. They were out in the middle of nowhere at the festival grounds. He was her ride home. This wasn't exactly an area she could rely on car service. She was going to have to face him again and speak to him if she wanted to go home. He would have questions. He deserved answers.

It was time to swallow her pride and go speak to him. Make up some excuse to... Laurel figured the only way to get through it was to *fake it until she could make it.* So, she pretended to have confidence she didn't own and that she wasn't completely mortified by what had just happened and started walking toward him.

Halfway there, she heard the sound of metal scraping cement. She glanced toward the noise in time to see that a metal basket from one of the kiddie rides had come loose and was barreling toward her, skidding across the cement. Sparks flew.

Griff must have jumped into action because as she tried to leap out of the way—realizing she was about to be smashed anyway—she received a push that allowed her to narrowly escape the blunt force of the cart.

It slammed into a metal light pole, cracking it in half and scattering the small group of folks that had gathered around the exit. Relief that she'd narrowly escaped being hit, was quickly replaced with panic that someone else might not have been so lucky. She skimmed the area for any signs of panic on any nearby faces and saw nothing, other than folks grabbing their children and scurrying far enough away to be out of the way in case of another incident.

No one was hurt. The worst Laurel took was an elbow scrape on the concrete to the backdrop of ear-piercing screams. As she scrambled to her feet, she saw that Griff had taken off after a pair of teenagers who'd broken into a full run. If he hadn't been there, she would have been crushed by the cart and it would be unfair to bolt out of sight without thanking him, despite her flee response kicking into high gear.

And then the reality of the situation smacked her in the face. Had someone just made an attempt to kill her?

As she followed Griff, she searched for a familiar face in the crowd. Had he found her? Ricky Harris would have a whole lot of resources at his disposal and he'd already proved to be fine with breaking the law despite being a cop. She scanned the faces looking for James too. After all, he'd been the one to visit the diner. Was he carrying out Timothy's cousin's work?

By the time Laurel caught up to Griff, he had both teens face down on the concrete. Laurel searched all the faces around them, looking for someone she recognized from back home. In her mind, there was no possible way this could have been an accident—even though she had no idea what the teenagers' involvement was or why they'd bolted in the first place.

Everyone had moved out of the way but no one else had taken off, running for their lives.

"One of you had better start talking or I'll arrest you both right here and now," Griff said to the lanky teens.

"Please. Please. We didn't know that was going to happen. We thought it was a prank. We didn't know anyone could get hurt. We thought we were playing a prank on someone. The ride wasn't supposed to break," one of the teens said through tears, his face twisted in what looked like absolute fear and anguish.

Both of the teens were visibly shaking at this point and even though their faces were mostly facing the cement, she could see their expressions along with puddles of tears.

One by one, Griff grabbed them by the elbow and pulled them up to a sitting position.

"Put your hands on top of your head where I can see 'em," Griff demanded.

Both complied.

"What's your name?" he asked the older-looking teen.

"Ethan, sir," he responded.

"Last name?" Griff asked.

"Smith," Ethan said, his voice shaking. "Am I under arrest?"

"No," Griff asked. "But it would be in your best interest to start explaining what just happened."

Ethan nodded. "This is my friend Alex Tindell," Ethan said.

Griff glanced over at the younger teen, who looked to be in shock.

"Do either one of you have any weapons on you, or am I about to find anything else that's going to incriminate you?" he asked.

"No, sir," Ethan said.

Alex was vigorously shaking his head as a small crowd formed and cell phones came out.

"I swear on my mother's life that we had no idea pulling that pin was going to break the ride. Some dude walked past us and dared us to do it," Ethan said. "We were just being stupid and doing it for attention. If anyone is hurt. Oh my God."

More tears spilled out as Ethan's face twisted in pure agony.

"How old are you guys?" Griff asked.

"Eighteen and sixteen," Ethan said, indicating he was the oldest.

"Tell me more about the dude," Griff said to Ethan. Of the pair of teens, he had the most composure.

"Some random dude," the older one said. "He walked right behind us and dared us to pull the pin out."

"Can you describe him?" Griff said, pulling out his phone and taking down a few notes.

Laurel held her breath waiting for the answer.

CHAPTER NINE

"No, sir," Ethan responded to Griff's question. He could almost feel the tension rising in Laurel. Clearly, she believed her life was in danger and this incident was aimed at her.

Out of the corner of Griff's eye, he saw Jonas Schneider barreling toward them with his gaze fixated on the teens. The event manager's hands were fisted at his sides and his cheeks were blood red. Everything about his body language said he was about to go after the teens. Griff needed to stop Jonas before he did something he would regret.

Griff shot a warning look at the teens.

"Do not move," he warned. Then, he turned toward the storm coming right at him that was Jonas. Griff purposely blocked Jonas's line of sight to the teens. They'd done something incredibly stupid, but based on their reaction so far, Griff believed the boys were unaware of the consequences of their actions and truly didn't mean to injure anyone.

"Hold on there a minute, Jonas," Griff said, holding his arms out.

Jonas's gaze was practically boring a hole through Griff to get to the teens. "I'll handle this one," Jonas said. The man was coming at those teens like a bull that saw red.

"You have every right to speak to those boys when I'm finished with them," Griff said, literally catching the man in time to redirect them both with a quick change in momentum in another direction. Anger rolled off Jonas in palpable waves.

Griff glanced over at Laurel who was sitting down, legs folded while watching over the teens. The two made eye contact for the briefest of moments, before she resumed scanning the faces of the gathering crowd.

He immediately realized she was looking for someone. It had happened before she'd bolted, when she fell over the stroller. Griff really hoped that when the dust settled, Laurel would trust him enough to sit down and have a conversation with him about what was putting that fear in her eyes. But right now, his sole focus had to be on keeping Jonas from taking out his fury on those teens.

"I appreciate what you're doing here, Griff. But I'm guessing, based on what I've been told, that those teens are responsible for putting people's lives in danger," Jonas said.

"I'm guessing no one was seriously injured," Griff said.

"No. Not technically, unless you count my insurance that's going to go up and the damage to the confidence good people have in me and the trust they put in me to keep them safe," Jonas said as he started pacing back and forth. His hands were secured on his waistband. Every few steps he tugged his trousers up.

"No one was injured. I know this whole incident probably scared a lot of folks, and I have every intention of putting out a statement that says the festival is in no way at fault. I will further say that a ride was tampered with by juveniles and that all safety standards have been met and exceeded for rides this year, just like in years past," Griff promised. He exhaled a little bit more in the knowledge that no one was hurt. There was a huge sense of relief with the revelation. "Based on what the kids have said so far, which I fully intend to investigate and check out, they acted stupid. Like teens are known to do from time to time. Which in no way excuses their behavior, but it does explain how this kind of thing happened. They will be punished for the stupidity. Rest assured, as scared as those kids are right now, they'll never do anything like this ever again."

"You bet they won't. Both with be banned for life from this festival. I don't ever want to see either one of their faces here again," Jonas said.

"Fair enough," Griff said. "No one would blame you for taking action to protect your festival, your customers, and your employees."

"That's exactly what I intend to do," Jonas said; a little bit of his fury was starting to ease. It was like their conversation was offering a slow release valve.

Jonas issued a sharp sigh.

"I'll do my best to make sure your insurance doesn't go up," Griff stated.

"I appreciate it, Sheriff. I really do," Jonas said. "But

we both know this kind of thing can ruin a festival forever. It could dry up business and send me into bankruptcy."

"We won't let that happen," Griff stated.

Jonas took another lap before shaking out his hands. "Okay," he said.

"Good. Now, let me go do my job while you go make sure Deputy Rustler has arrived on scene. If not, see to it no one touches anything so we can see about lifting fingerprints until he gets there, or I return. Preserve the area for me, okay?" Griff fished his cell out of his pocket before looking up. "I'd also like the space where they pulled the pin cordoned off."

Jonas was nodding his head in agreement. At least Griff seemed to be getting through to the man.

"I'll circle back with you once I get more details from the boys," Griff stated. "You have my word."

"Good enough," Jonas said after a thoughtful pause.

They shook hands before heading in opposite directions. Griff texted Deputy Rustler to let him know what was coming. His deputy had already reached out to Griff to let him know he was at the sight of the incident.

By the time Griff returned to the teens, they had their IDs out and ready for him. Griff figured Laurel had something to do with that. They were also a whole lot calmer and seemed to have been able to dry their tears.

"I swear we didn't know this would happen," Alex said with wide eyes. "We didn't think anyone could get hurt."

Griff had dealt with enough young people to realize

it was sometimes difficult for them to consider all the possible consequences ahead of time.

"He just walked right past," Ethan said. "He sounded like Greer's cousin."

"What's Greer's last name?" Griff asked.

"Barber," Ethan offered.

"Do you have a phone number for him?" Griff asked, thinking they might be able to clear this up with a phone call and find the person responsible.

Ethan shook his head. "I have Greer's number in my contacts," Ethan supplied, motioning toward the phone in front of him that was sitting on the pavement.

"I want you to call him," Griff stated. He didn't need to look at Laurel to realize she hoped this could be explained by a teenage prank. There was also a whole lot of doubt in her eyes. A quick glance in her direction and he saw the tension in her shoulders, the defiance in her eyes, and the sheer bravery being displayed at her sticking around instead of bolting like she most likely wanted to do.

"What should I say?" Ethan asked.

"I want you to ask if he knows where his cousin is. Make up an excuse as to why you're asking," Griff instructed.

"Okay," Ethan said.

Griff hoped it would be this easy to clear up who was responsible for urging the teens to remove the pin. They'd said it sounded like their friend's cousin, and if their friend and his cousin were older, Griff could see how they would do most anything to look cool in Greer's eyes. It didn't mean they were off the hook. They were both in trouble, but the fact they were cooperating would go a long way toward him recommending leniency versus asking the judge to make an example out of them.

Ethan pulled up Greer's contact and then tapped the screen. He started to put the cell to his ear and then seemed to think better of it when he brought it down and hit the speaker. His eyes flashed at Griff.

"Call him how you normally do and try not to sound suspicious," Griff stated.

Ethan nodded.

"What's up, dude?" a male voice stated.

"Hey, Greer," Ethan said. "I was just calling...I was pretty sure that I just saw your cousin at the festival, but he walked by so fast I couldn't be a hundred percent. Are you guys here? Cuz, I was thinking maybe we could hook up."

Griff was impressed with Ethan's composure and thought the kid was handling himself quite well under the pressure. Then again, it was probably the pressure that had him digging deep to pull this one out.

"Nah, Robbie couldn't possibly be at the festival because he's sitting right next to..." Greer released a loud groan. The background noise indicated he was playing some kind of video game and had just lost. "You jerk. How did you pull that off?" There was a beat of silence before Greer returned to the call in progress.

The theory this was someone familiar to them just went down the toilet. Another flash of fear passed behind Laurel's eyes when she brought her gaze to Griff's. She immediately looked away as if she didn't want to give away her reaction to the news.

"Okay. Cool. I guess it wasn't him then," Ethan said.

"Wait. Hold on. How long are you planning on sticking around?" Greer asked.

"Not that much longer. It's getting boring. Don't even worry about trying to show up. By the time you get here, we'll be on our way home anyway," Ethan said. "I just thought if you guys were already here, we could hang out. It's getting lame."

"We'll be here all day if you want to swing by," Greer said.

Griff didn't want to say they would probably still be sitting on that exact same spot on the couch three or four hours later playing those same video games, but it was true.

"Okay. Cool. Talk to you later." Ethan ended the call. He looked up at Griff and said, "I could have sworn it was Robbie."

"There were a lot of people around. I'm sure you just heard what you wanted to," Griff said.

"Are we going to jail?" Alex asked. He'd been intensely working the hem of his shirt in between the thumb and forefinger in his left hand, a nervous tick.

"You did something stupid and criminal. People could have died. This is serious and you should be scared right now. There are a couple of things working in your favor. Number one, you are cooperating. Number two, no one was injured. This is beyond a prank and I want you both to understand the seriousness of what could have happened. Since it didn't, you are going to get a break and likely be charged with criminal mischief," Griff said. "Don't ever let me see you doing anything like this ever again. And, between you and me, if that's the kind of cousin your friend has, you'd be smart to steer clear of him too."

"Yes, sir," Ethan said as he nodded.

"Sit tight while I call my deputy and have him come over to process you both. It'll be up to him whether or not he lets you go or writes you up, but I will have a conversation with him and let him know how cooperative you were. We'll go from there," Griff said. He wanted to know a little more about them, so he could pass over the information to his deputy. Plus, he wanted more information to make a determination for himself as to whether or not these young people truly deserved leniency. "What kind of grades do you get in school?"

"As and Bs," Alex offered almost immediately. He was dressed in a rock t-shirt and jeans. He was tall and lanky, not yet having grown into his frame.

"I used to get mostly Bs," Ethan admitted.

"What grade are you in?" Griff asked.

"I'm at the community college," Ethan said. "Trying to finish up my basics so I can transfer to a four-year program."

"I'm guessing you're a freshman," Griff stated.

"Yes, sir. And I work hard for the Bs I get."

Both of the teens had been nothing but respectful since Griff had called them out. When he'd first seen the expressions on their faces moments after the pin pulling incident, they'd been truly mortified.

Based on his assessment, these teens deserved a break. He pulled out his cell and communicated the message to his deputy to go as easy as possible. The teens were also going to have to apologize to Jonas, and he was going to be a tough sell on giving these kids a break. Maybe they would work off the damage they'd caused. The festival was open for a couple more days. Griff might be able to arrange for the teens to make restitution by pushing brooms or emptying trash.

"I'm not making any promises here, but would the two of you be able to come back tomorrow and the next day to work if I was able to work something out with the event manager?" Griff asked.

"Yes, sir," Ethan said. "You tell us when to be here and we'll show."

"Okay," Griff stated. He could work with them, considering their attitudes were in the right place. People made mistakes. Young, impressionable people were high on the list of mistake-makers. Their brains weren't fully developed yet and that wasn't helping with the impulsive bad decisions. He'd learned that attitude made all the difference. He'd had true juvenile delinquents sitting across the room from him. He could generally tell by looking at their posture how the discussion was going to go. They had angry eyes and usually folded their arms over their chest with their chin up like they were daring Griff to throw a punch. Those meetings didn't tend to go well. When kids felt like the whole world had abandoned them, they had nothing to lose and cooperating with a sheriff was the last thing on their mind. They usually came across like they had a chip on their shoulders the size of a Buick and said as few words as possible.

The teens' eyes were wide open with fear, which told Griff they weren't used to getting into trouble. They came across as genuine and scared. The fact they cared about getting good grades in school painted a picture that they wanted to take care of their responsibilities and most likely had some pride in their work.

He'd come across far too many broken teens with dead eyes and a bad attitude in his career. Ethan and Alex didn't fit into that category. These two truly did come across as naïve enough to follow someone's dare on the spur of the moment, especially since they truly believed they knew the person. Getting caught was probably the best thing that would happen to them, because it would scare them into learning the lesson.

Deputy Rustler responded with a text, saying he would take care of the situation and was on his way over. One glance at Laurel caused all Griff's protective instincts to surface. Granted, she'd been doing an amazing job of taking care of herself, but he needed to know who put the fear in her eyes and could only hope she would tell him.

Rustler arrived as Griff asked the teens to stand.

"Take care of these guys for me," Griff said to Rustler after giving his statement. And then he turned to Laurel. "Are you ready to get out of here?"

"Yes," she responded, and there was something very concerning in her tone of voice.

———

Laurel followed Griff to his truck in silence as she searched every face looking for one of Timothy's colleagues. She had no idea if James or Ricky had found her. Or if they would, now that she'd become news. With everyone having cell phones and social media at their fingertips, it was getting harder and harder to disappear into the shadows.

Most of her place was packed up in a suitcase and a couple of small bags. It hadn't taken long and it was a shame her life had been reduced to such a small imprint. Tears welled in her eyes but she refused to let them fall. What good would crying do anyway? It wouldn't change her circumstances or the fact she needed to make her exit without saying goodbye to Mrs. Brubaker.

That was the worst part, having to slink out of town like a common criminal, without saying goodbye to the few people she cared about. Leaving Marissa and the twins had been one of the most difficult decisions to make. Not being able to tell her best friend that she was going had gutted her. No goodbye.

It was for Marissa's benefit, and Laurel would do the same all over again to keep her friend out of it. Marissa was too nice to say, but she'd been on the receiving end of snide remarks around town for her association with Laurel.

Plus, Marissa would have done her best to talk Laurel out of going. Leaving had been difficult enough. There'd been no reason to drag it out when there was nothing Marissa could have done to change Laurel's mind.

Shoulders back, Laurel walked to the passenger side of the truck. Griff seemed to respect her privacy, not asking what was going through her mind. He'd been good about it, considering the fact he had to have loads of questions by now. Having someone paid to make keen observations probably hadn't been the best choice for a date today.

Except that Griff was special.

Laurel really had hoped the dare issued to the teens would have come from someone they knew. It would be so simple if that was the case, and Laurel might actually consider staying in town another couple of days. There was an unfamiliar pull toward Griff, like magnet to steel, and nothing like her relationships in the past. Then again, *this* was nothing more than two random people who'd met, experienced off-the-charts chemistry, and then life forced them to go separate ways.

It happened. Right? There'd be others like this in the future. Right? There'd be a time when she could put down roots again. Right?

She climbed into the cab of the truck, letting Griff open and shut the door for her. The idea of leaving Gunner hit harder than expected. *Suck it up.*

The ride home was silent and there was something she couldn't quite put her finger on that had been building since the moment she clicked her seatbelt on. Griff pulled up beside the cabin and, she realized, didn't cut off the engine.

"I would like to come inside, have a cup of coffee, and talk," he finally said after what seemed like thoughtful consideration. "The last thing I want to do is make you uncomfortable or feel like I'm making demands. You have every right to leave things right here. But this, whatever *this* is that seems to be happening between us, would feel unfinished. At least to me, and it might be my ego talking here, but I believe you feel the same."

He kept his hand on the wheel and his gaze steadfast on the stretch of lake in front of him.

"You're not wrong, Griff. But it's complicated. *I'm* complicated," she admitted and felt warmth crawl up her neck and then focus on her cheeks, heating them six shades past red.

"I can't do complicated," he said so quickly she believed him. "But I need honesty, or it won't work."

A few moments of silence passed before either spoke again.

"I like you, Laurel. That doesn't happen a whole lot to me," he said. "And I think you like me too. It would be a shame to waste whatever it is brewing between us. I'm not eighteen anymore and I know the qualities I'm looking for. No one ticks the boxes quite like you. So, I'm asking you to give me tonight. Not your whole life. Not even tomorrow. Give me this evening so we can finish our date properly. And then you can finish packing and move on."

Laurel gasped.

Then she realized, of course, he'd seen the state of her bathroom. Plus, she'd accidentally left the door to her bedroom open; he didn't seem like the type to snoop around but he'd walked right past the room twice.

"You're trouble, Griff Quinn," she said.

"I sure hope so," was all he said in response.

Now, she had to make a choice. Let him in and risk more of her heart, or tell him to go, and quite possibly never feel like this with another human being for the rest of her life.

CHAPTER TEN

"Take your time deciding. I can wait."

Griff genuinely had no idea which way this was headed. The pull he felt toward the person in the seat next to him was being experienced on more levels than he could count. At the top sat his attraction to Laurel. Her mind, her attitude, and...well...her body. Next on the list was the fact their date had been interrupted, and he wanted to see where it would have taken them. And then there was the fact that she seemed ready to jump out of her skin, and all he wanted to do was to fix everything, so she never felt so scared again. The intensity of that pull unnerved him.

And yet, being with her made him feel like he was exactly where he should be.

"I make a good cup of coffee," she said without making eye contact.

Was going inside a good idea? Probably not. Would it stop him? Definitely not.

"Okay, I'm always up for a good cup of coffee." He exited the driver's seat and came around to the passenger's side, before opening the door for her.

"Thanks," she said to him. He must have shot her quite the look because she quickly added, "For trying to give me something normal."

A twig snapped in the scrub brush nearby. Laurel gasped and her hand immediately came up to clutch her chest. Griff's gaze flew to the area, homing in on anything that moved. A small jackrabbit sprang from the thicket, bolting across the dirt road behind the cabin.

Laurel's instantaneous reaction told him she'd been at this for a while. She'd been conditioned to jump at every noise so much so that it was habit at this point.

"Let's go inside," he said, thinking they were too out in the open standing there. Basically, they were sitting ducks for anyone with a long-range rifle. Plus, he wanted to secure the inside before checking out what might have caused the jackrabbit to bolt like that.

Laurel nodded and then walked toward the door. She unlocked the deadbolt. He'd noticed it when she came out. His buddy had never felt the need to sew up a cabin so tightly before.

"I asked for a security system," Laurel said.

"I'm guessing that was a no," he stated as she opened the door and led them inside.

"A hard no," she said on a sigh.

She closed and deadbolted the door behind them, before leading the way into the kitchen.

"Feel free to have a seat," she said, motioning toward the table.

"Mind if I stand up?" he asked.

She stared at him for a long moment like she was sizing up his intentions.

"The window over the sink gives me a good view of the area the jackrabbit bolted from. I'd like to keep an eye on it, and since you locked the deadbolt, I'm guessing you also don't want to be alone in the house right now," he surmised before folding his arms over his chest. "Is that right or completely off base?"

"It's dead on," she admitted as she went to work fixing coffee. "Feel free to stand or sit anywhere you want. I trust you."

Griff figured those last three words didn't come easily to her.

"Thank you for the confidence," he stated as he kept one eye on the thicket. If anything else moved out there, the deadbolt would hold him back at least a few seconds. It would take another fifteen to twenty to cut across the lane. So, basically, he'd be at a twenty-five to thirty-second disadvantage. He did, however, know this area like the back of his hand.

"You're welcome," she said, handing over a fresh mug. "Black?"

"Yes," he said.

Laurel fixed her own cup before sitting down at the table.

"See anything out there?" she asked after taking a sip.

"No." He barely got out the word when he saw a flash, like sun glinting off metal. "Hold on."

He bolted toward the front door and then bent

down to withdraw his weapon from his ankle holster while she unbolted the lock.

"Stay inside unless I say otherwise," he said to her as he palmed his backup weapon. "Okay?"

"Got it. Believe me, I'm not going anywhere near the door until you come back and that's only to let you in," she said, opening the door.

He pressed a brief kiss to her lips in answer before taking off. There was no need to remind her to lock the door behind him. She had it down pat. His muscles tensed at the trauma she had to have experienced in order to think it was a good idea to live like this.

Griff reminded himself to take a breath as he sprinted toward the tree line. He led with his weapon, unlike those cop shows where the director wanted a clear view of the actor's face for the camera. In the real world of law enforcement, the eyes followed a direct line of sight extending from the tip of the barrel. The couple of seconds this position shaved off could easily mean the difference between life and death.

Running directly toward the flash of metal, Griff maintained focus on the area, while continuously scanning the tree line. He reached the thicket and then started weaving through the trees until he made it to the exact spot the flash had come from. There was no reason for there to be metal here. At least, nothing in nature. Someone had to have been here and just a few minutes ago.

Whoever it was, was gone now.

Griff surveyed the area. He dropped down and scanned the scrub brush looking for any evidence. Then, he heard the snap of a tree branch roughly twenty yards ahead. His instincts told him to run toward the noise, but that would take him even farther away from the cabin. It occurred to him someone could have been drawing him away from Laurel. This could have been part of a grand scheme to separate the two of them. Taking her out would be a whole lot easier that way. Of course, that wasn't the only possibility. Still, he didn't want to risk it.

Rather than run off half-cocked into the woods, he decided to double back and make sure she was good. The cabin lock would offer enough protection for him to have time to sprint back. Since he didn't see anything move out here, he headed toward the cabin.

The door cracked open the second his boot hit the porch. Laurel rushed him inside.

"Did you see anyone?" she asked, bolting the deadbolt behind him.

"I heard something and I'm one hundred percent certain someone was out there," he said, returning to the kitchen where he'd set down his coffee after tucking his backup weapon in his ankle holster. "Tell me who it is."

"I don't know," she said, shaking her head. "Believe me, I would gladly tell you if I could be certain."

"Then, tell me why anyone would be out there in the first place," he pressed.

She hesitated.

"I can't help if I don't know who or what I'm dealing with," he stated. This was it. This was the moment she had to decide if she was going to let him in, or if she was going to keep the wall up and give him very little to go on.

"I should probably just take off like I'd planned to, once it's clear," she said on a sharp sigh. Nothing in her body language said she wanted to take that course of action.

"And what would that do?" he asked, figuring it was time to put the cards on the table in a manner of speaking. "Won't he just follow you?"

She bit down on her bottom lip.

"He will, and I think you know it," he said. And then asked, "What number is this?"

Her eyebrows drew together.

"How many towns have you been to? How many times have you uprooted yourself because of this... what?...ex-boyfriend? Husband?" he asked.

She shook her head.

"He wasn't my husband," she said. "We'd only been dating a few months when I realized I was in over my head with this guy."

Griff took a sip of coffee and leaned forward, resting his elbows against the table's edge.

"That's when I decided to end it with him," she continued.

"But he didn't see the relationship as over," Griff said, when she seemed unable to say the words out loud.

"No. He didn't," she said before slowly exhaling. "He told me that he would decide when he was done with me. Then, he grabbed me by the wrists and yanked me down the hall and into the bedroom."

Her gaze unfocused, almost as though she was looking inside herself for the right words. Or maybe she was just avoiding eye contact while talking about what had probably been the most traumatic day of her life.

As much as Griff disliked this part while doing his job, it was necessary for him to assess a threat and get enough information to search for a perp. It had to be done.

"We'd never...at least...not yet," she said. "But he decided we were going to despite my attempts break free from his grip." Laurel took a sip of coffee and then rolled the mug around in her hands. She seemed to need to take a breather before moving on.

After a few deep breaths, she continued, "When I fought back and shouted at him to stop, he threatened me."

"I'm sorry you had to go through something no one should ever have to face," he said and hated how painful it must be to relive the experience again.

Laurel glanced up and then locked eyes with him for a brief moment before looking away, but her appreciation for his comment shone through.

"He pulled a knife from inside his jacket pocket," she continued. "I had no idea it was there and immediately asked him to put it away. Shock doesn't begin to describe my reaction." She stared at a spot on the wall. "He was unfazed. Nothing I said helped. It only made him angrier." She paused for a couple of beats. "I'd never seen that kind of rage staring back at me. And for what? Because I didn't want to date him any longer? My brain couldn't fathom what was happening. If it could... if I'd known...let's just say I would have handled the whole situation differently."

Griff had sat on this side of a conversation like this many times during his career. It never got easier hearing the stories. He realized he was gripping the coffee mug tight enough to crack it if he didn't let up.

"The next thing I knew the knife was at my throat and I went into panic mode," she said. "He told me to undress and lie on the bed. I had no idea what he was going to do to me but there was a look in his eyes that I'd never seen before and I never want to see again in another human being. In fact, it didn't seem human at all." A shiver rocked her body. "I think I blanked out on much of the rest of the details to be honest, and it happened almost three years ago, so things are definitely more of a blur now. But we struggled for the knife and he ended up stabbed instead of me. I don't even know how it happened exactly. I had a black eye for a while from an elbow. At least I think it was an elbow. It's strange the kinds of details I remember. Like the fact he was wearing a leather bomber jacket that night, but I couldn't tell you if he had on pants let alone if he had on jeans or dress slacks."

"It's a survival mechanism," Griff reassured. He realized there was more to the story as she bit down on her bottom lip again. His heart already went out to her.

"He was already gone before the ambulance arrived," she said. "There was so much blood. I thought I'd never wash it all off." Her eyes glittered like she was about to cry but her chin came up instead. Determination caused her to keep going. Her strength was one of many traits that had drawn him to her.

Griff had seen trauma like this from abusive relationships. He'd witnessed the shock in someone's eyes when they realized they'd accidentally taken a life. He'd followed up on cases, sat through trials, and heard about the nightmares that followed cases like these. It was gut-wrenching to hear and never got easier. The fact he cared made him good at his job.

Laurel issued a sharp sigh.

"The ordeal itself was bad enough and I thought the worst was over," she said.

"The trial?" he asked, hating how a victim could be revictimized during a court trial. He could only imagine how horrific it must be for victims to have to relieve the worst day of their lives when all they probably wanted to do was forget and find a way to move on.

"Yes, but the harassment was worse," she stated.

"Harassment?" he repeated, not liking the sound of the word.

"Timothy..." She flashed eyes at Griff. "That was his name."

Griff nodded.

"Timothy was from a prominent family," she started. "His cousin was a cop. His buddies were on the wrong side of the law. I know that now, but didn't when we first met."

"There are criminals who are very good at hiding their activities from everyone, including their family," he said. He'd seen it many times. The shocked look on a family member's face when he asked them to come in for an interview; vouching for a loved one, only to find out they'd been covering, thinking they were doing them a favor.

"Timothy was very smooth," she stated. "Initially, I was charged with involuntary manslaughter. My lawyer said evidence of crimes were found in Timothy's house when the cops searched his place, but it was all deemed inadmissible. We requested a change of venue when he discovered the judge was a golfing buddy of Timothy's father."

"I'm guessing that was shot down fast," he said.

She nodded. Some of the spark returned to her eyes.

"There was no denying that it was self-defense. Luckily, one of my neighbors overheard the fighting. People usually stick to their own business, but he's an older gentleman that I used to shop for when he needed things and couldn't get out. He vouched for me. Timothy's fingerprints were the only ones on the knife handle. He was larger than me and stronger. He'd been working out and taking steroids to buff up, unbeknownst to me at the time, but they also seemed to give him quite a temper," she said. "It all came out during the investigation but many of the details were suppressed at the trial."

With all the information available about steroid use, Griff was surprised to hear folks still used them. He shook his head, unable to find the right words to offer comfort, so he just listened.

"His cousin didn't stop harassing me and neither did his friends, or the rest of the town for that matter. I was released from jail quickly but it took a long time to go to trial because the courts were backlogged. I'd been ordered to stay in town but it was next to impossible to go anywhere without someone getting in my face, whispering behind my back, or my tires 'randomly' getting slit in a parking lot," she said.

"It sounds like you were living in a nightmare. I've heard about these things happening but I've never spoken to someone it happened to personally," he said to her before reaching over to touch her hand in order to offer some comfort.

Given all she'd been through, he was surprised she didn't pull away. But then, he hoped she felt the same electricity he did every time they touched. And he also hoped he was a safety net for her.

————

Laurel hadn't spoken about the events of that fateful night in years, and she'd only described the night in court. Her attorney had advised her to keep a tight lid on the events and speak to as few people as possible while he tried to attain a venue change. She had done as requested, even dodging questions from Marissa about what had happened. All her best friend knew was what she'd read. Talking about it should make Laurel sick, except that Griff had a way of making her feel at ease and able to keep going.

"Timothy's family was able to keep much of the details out of the news and, to be honest, I was way out of my league going up against them and their attorneys in tailored suits. Money was no object and they wanted me to pay dearly for their only son's death. So, I was grateful the jury sided with me in the end," she admitted.

"As they should have," Griff stated with a fire in his eyes. Someone as honest and honorable as him would take great offense to the system being manipulated and used to harm victims, when it should stick to punishing criminals. His thoughts were clear in his tense and concerned expression, and the way he ground his back teeth.

"The whole process was drawn out, and then life was awful for me after I was deemed innocent and it was declared that I acted in self-defense," she said. "I imagine Timothy's family was fired up after the jury decision."

"I'm surprised the judge didn't force them to deliberate longer," he said.

"He did," she admitted. "Having someone who is supposed to uphold the law and protect victims force them back into their chamber was horrific."

"Should have never happened," Griff stated. "There are jerks who are supposed to be upholding the law and aren't. They make it so much more difficult on those of us who are in this job for the right reasons."

"I remember being scared the jury would change their minds, but they didn't," she said. "In fact, they read a statement condemning the judge for making the request in the first place."

"At least they saw what was happening," he said before adding, "you should have never been subjected to that level of injustice."

His hand closed around hers. Contact sent her heart racing, as warmth spread through her. There was a time not so long ago that she feared she would never welcome a man's touch again. She went through a period when she believed Timothy had ripped that from her completely after what had happened. In the couple of years that followed, the last thing she wanted was to be alone with a man.

But being with Griff was a different story. She

wanted to be in his company. Talking to him came easily and telling him her story had made the boulder that had been docked on her chest lift.

There was a lightness to her now that she hadn't experienced in years, possibly even before the assault.

"Timothy's parents didn't want him going down in history as someone who would commit rape," she finally said. Those words spoken aloud were so freeing tears sprang to her eyes. "This might sound off the wall, but I never thought I'd say any of those words out loud."

"Why is that?" Griff asked with concern in his voice.

"I trained myself not to speak of the horrors that happened that night and I'm realizing that by keeping them locked inside me, I've robbed myself of the ability to move on from it," she said. "Because I feel like this huge weight has been lifted while talking to you."

"That's good," he said to her. His masculine voice traveled over her and through her, awakening places she's suppressed far too long.

"It feels good," she said.

"Can I make a suggestion?" he asked.

"Sure," she said.

"Speak to a professional, as well," he offered. "No one should have to go through an experience like the one you survived. You're a survivor and it's clear to see that you're a strong person. I have a deep respect and admiration for your strength. It's also my experience strong people are the last ones to seek help."

She nodded. Those words hit home.

"I've been thinking that once I settle down, I'd like to do just that," she admitted.

"I know of a few very good therapists not far from

Gunner that I could recommend. And if you don't end up settling here, they could refer you to someone at your next stop," he said.

"I'd like that a lot actually," she said, thinking how wonderful it would be to truly move on from the ordeal at some point in the future. To feel whole again, like she was beginning to while she was around the sheriff. But whole in a way she'd never experienced before. Laurel had never believed meeting someone would complete her. She was already a complete person. So, maybe 'complete' was the wrong word. Compliment seemed like a better choice. No one had ever complimented her in the way Griff Quinn did.

"Can I ask a question?" he continued.

"Go ahead," she said, unsure of what would come next. And yet, something changed inside her in the last couple of minutes. Something she wanted to understand and explore.

"When do you plan to leave town?" he asked before linking their fingers. She liked having physical contact with Griff. There was something about his touch that kept her nerves a few notches below panic even under the most intense moments.

This was where it became sticky because she wasn't used to detailing out her plans with anyone.

She shrugged.

"You have a timeline," he said. "And, quite possibly, a destination in mind. I'm not asking for the latter because it wouldn't be fair to you, and you will most likely be moving around for a bit."

She nodded.

"All I'm asking is when you plan to go," he said, and it was impossible to resist answering.

"I'm planning to leave tonight," she admitted. "Or, I should say that I *was*."

"What changed your mind?" he asked.

"To be honest...*you*." There. She'd said it. She'd said the words. He now knew she was developing feelings for him in the short time they'd been together.

"Would you consider sticking around longer?" he asked.

"It's too risky," she said, leaving off the fact she would like nothing more than to put down roots in Gunner. "Could you do me a favor, though?"

"Anything. Name it." The fact he didn't hesitate caused her to wish life could be different.

"I'm not going to have a chance to say goodbye to Mrs. Brubaker and she has been so nice to me," she said. "She reminds me of someone who was very special to me."

Laurel expected questions. She'd opened a topic and didn't explain.

"Done," he confirmed without blinking.

"You don't mind?" she asked, still a little stunned at the rapid response.

"I'm one hundred percent certain she would love to hear it from you and I'll likely be a disappointment for an exchange, but I'll stop by tomorrow and explain that you had a family emergency and needed to leave town immediately," he said. "Do you want me to ask for your last check?"

"You would do that for me?" she asked. There was

no reason he should cover for her except that he was genuinely a good human being.

"Of course," he said like it was nothing. But it wasn't nothing. And for reasons she couldn't immediately understand or rationalize, she began to cry.

Laurel stood up and walked out of the room, Griff's voice calling after her.

CHAPTER ELEVEN

The puzzle pieces clicked together in Griff's mind. Laurel was on the run from a terrible situation...person. He was unclear as to who was after her. Was it the cop who'd harassed her? The anger simmering in Griff's chest that came with the knowledge a cop would pull something like this, almost bubbled over.

Again, he was impressed by Laurel's strength. She'd been through situations no one should have to and she'd managed to come out stronger on the other side. Some used these kinds of setbacks as an excuse to give up. Not Laurel.

"Sorry, I had to catch my breath for a minute," she said as she returned. Her eyes were red and just a little puffy. It made him want to reach out to her and be her comfort.

"No need to apologize," he reassured.

"I'm not a crier, so..."

"Tell me more about what you think happened today at the festival," he said, moving on so she didn't feel the need to explain. She had every right to cry and even more rights to take a few minutes for herself.

"Ricky Harris is the cop from home, who could still be after me," she said. "He has considerable resources at his disposal and he's the one who threatened me. He blasted into my kitchen and backed me up against the wall. Told me I would regret what I did to his cousin."

"The rapist?" he asked, not bothering to hide his frustration that one of his own could be dirty. He knew it happened and he'd heard specific stories but it never got easier.

Laurel nodded.

Griff's hands fisted. He flexed and released his fingers a couple of times to ease some of the tension. "He has no business in my county," he ground out. In his mind, the incident at the festival really could have been a prank. And yet, she seemed to have a very firm opinion it wasn't.

"There's another person too," she continued. "His name is James Whitney and he was Timothy's best friend. They were close. He found me at a diner where I got a job in the first city after leaving Chicago. My house had been broken into and he'd threatened that I would meet with an 'accident'."

"You believe he broke into your home to set something up," he said.

"That's right," she said. "Bricks had been thrown in my windows. I can't count the number of times my car was vandalized. It could be parked in broad daylight but no one ever seemed to witness any of it. I have no doubt someone had entered my home to set up a homicide to look like an accident. The cops would have closed the book without much of an investigation if something had happened to me."

Griff muttered a few choice words.

"I knew I had to get out of Chicago after the threat. I'm sure James was working with Ricky to find me, but of course, I have no proof," she said on a sharp sigh.

"Do you have pictures of these men?" Griff asked.

"I can probably find something online," she confirmed. "But what does it matter if I'm gone?"

"They come here for you, I want to know about it," he stated. "Everything that happens in my county is my business."

"Okay," she said and there was a spark of something in her eyes. Hope?

"You seem surprised by my offer to help," he said.

"No one has had my back in a very long time," she admitted. "I had a best friend back home who would have, but I couldn't risk her being dragged into this. She's the mother of twins and her babies needed her more than I did."

"Who protected you?" he asked.

"Me," she said on a shrug. "It's just been me, figuring it out along the way and making all kinds of mistakes. But I'm still here, so that's probably a good thing."

"If you don't mind me saying so, it sounds like a lonely journey," he said.

"It has been," she agreed. "But what else am I supposed to do? Put someone else in danger? End up with someone hurt in the crossfire? You saw what happened today. Anyone could have been hurt, or *worse*." Her body shivered as she spoke the words.

"I'm not convinced what happened today was

related yet," he said. "But someone has been watching the cabin and I intend to find out who."

"What if discovering the truth puts you in danger?" she asked.

"With all due respect, it's my job," he pointed out.

"That's fair," she conceded.

"What would you say if I personally asked you to stick around?" He figured it couldn't hurt to push his luck. She seemed determined to go and there was little he could do to stop her. First, she needed to know her options.

"I'm not sure, Griff," she started. "It's risky and you have to work, so you can't be around me twenty-four-seven."

"What if I can?" he asked. "I have time saved. I could put one of my deputies in charge for a few days until we sort this whole thing out."

"I can't ask that of you," she said. "You have a life here and I'm sure people need you."

"You need me too," he said.

She bit down on her bottom lip again and her gaze narrowed, a sure sign she was considering his request.

Their gazes met, and he held onto hers for a long moment before she finally shifted to staring at a spot on the wall.

"What makes you think today was a random prank?" she asked.

"First of all, we don't have evidence to prove otherwise," he pointed out.

"Okay," she said.

"And second of all, these things do happen. Around here, a prank is far more likely," he said.

"What about the person who seems to be watching the cabin?" she asked. "That can't be random."

"No, it can't," he said. "I'm trying to figure that one out and how it might be related but we don't have enough to go on."

She drummed her fingertips on the wooden table.

"There is a chance you've picked up a fan in Gunner," he said. "Fan is the wrong word. An interested party."

"That gives me the creeps," she said.

"Agreed." He paused. "You have been secretive and that might have caught the interest of local teens. Kids around here can get into all kinds of mischief, and spying on a newcomer who is private about her affairs isn't out of the realm of possibility."

"You got me there," she said. "If I was any person off the street, I would agree one hundred percent with what you're saying. My history has me thinking otherwise. The fact James tracked me down once already gives me the creeps and sends all my warning flares on high alert."

"After what you've been through, your response is more than reasonable," he said. "I'm looking at the situation from another perspective. One that hasn't been on the run for...how long?"

"Nine months," she supplied.

"With no end in sight," he said. "Because if James or Ricky followed you here after all this time, they won't stop until they find you. Then what?"

"An accident," she said. "Like they planned all along."

"If you leave here, you're on your own again," Griff said. "You'll be alone with no one to have your back."

"Only until they stop looking for me," she said.

"And when will that be?" he asked. "What happens when you let your guard down?"

Laurel sat there for a long moment. At least she hadn't immediately shot him down.

"Let me ask the question this way. Do you want to leave Gunner?" he asked.

A long pause was followed by one word. "No," she said.

"I can help you get your life back," he said. "If you'll allow me to help."

"What do you propose?" she asked.

"I'd like to quietly investigate the dirty cop for one," he said.

"I've already spoken to Chief Russo. He doesn't care. In fact, he told me that he couldn't protect me from accidents," she said. "He made it clear that he planned to look the other way if anything happened to me. He refused to investigate the break in and the bricks thrown through my windows. He said emotions were running high and he didn't have enough resources to watch over my place."

"This guy sounds like a class-A jerk," Griff pointed out.

"He was," she agreed.

"I can dig around without going through him. Normally, professional courtesy would dictate a call to the chief first, but this guy's dirty, so there's no use," he said.

Laurel reached out and placed a hand on Griff's

forearm. The now-familiar jolt of electricity rocketed through him, seeking an outlet.

"I'm not sure if I can stay here anymore," she said. "I'll jump at everything that makes a noise."

"You could stay with me," he said. "Not many folks are stupid enough to come at me where I live."

"What about my work?" she started.

"I can speak to your boss. See if I can arrange for time off."

"She won't go for it," she said. "I'll be fired. She's already made it clear that I'm expendable."

"Then, you won't be any worse off than if you leave town. Either way, you lose a job. If we go with my way, you have a shot at keeping one," he pointed out.

Laurel worked over her bottom lip.

"Have you had any contact with co-workers? Has anyone asked you out?" he asked, not wanting to admit how much he wanted to hear the answers to those questions.

"Tad Durant has been asking me out," she said. "I generally avoid him as much as possible, but he has been persistent."

"I know him," Griff stated, thinking Tad was a person of interest. Could it be him lurking in the trees? Laurel may not have outright rejected him, but he might have taken her disinterest personally. Tad didn't live in Gunner. He drove over from Barrel City, which was half an hour east of town. "At least, I know *of* him."

"There's something about him that I can't put my finger on," she said.

"When I swing by your work tomorrow, I can pull him aside and speak to him. At the very least, I can convince him that it's in his best interest to mind his own business when it comes to you," he said.

It annoyed Griff more than it should, that Tad seemed to have set his sights on Laurel. Strange, because she certainly didn't belong to Griff, no matter how strong the attraction between them was. Shame.

———

Did Laurel dare hope she could stay in Gunner?

Hope blossomed inside her chest for the first time in years, and she wanted to lean into it with every fiber of her being. Hope made her believe she wouldn't have to move again. Hope made her believe there would come a day in the very near future when she could go to the store without constantly looking over her shoulder. Hope had her thinking this could end. She reminded herself just how dangerous it could be.

"You said James is the one who visited you at the diner," Griff continued. "What happened?"

"I heard his voice, heard him asking about me and whether or not I worked there, and then I made a quick exit out the back door," she informed, thinking she'd had no plans to wait around and see what he wanted. She knew. He wanted her. Gone.

"What about your friend in Chicago?" he asked. "Have you been in contact with her over the past nine months?"

"No." She shook her head for emphasis. Missing Marissa was a physical ache. "There's no way I would risk it."

"The babies?" he asked, but it was more statement than question.

She nodded. "And her."

He seemed to understand.

"The harassment got to be awful for me. There was no way I was putting my friend through that. We'd been through too much together for me to bring that kind of trouble to her door," she explained.

"Sounds like the two of you go way back," he said.

"Best friends since the first day of fourth grade," she said. "I'd come to live with my grandmother after my mom disappeared. Courts may have been involved at some point but I honestly don't remember the details."

The look on his face said he assumed the worst.

"All I do know is that she left me willingly. Said it got to be too much to take care of me and that she deserved a life. I never met my real grandmother. The person I called grandmother was actually my great-grandmother, and she was an amazing person," she said. "I wish you could have met her."

"So do I," he stated with so much warmth and conviction more of those tears threatened.

Laurel wanted to lean into it, into Griff.

"She was an amazing person," Laurel said, picking back up on the conversation thread.

"Sounds like someone I would have gotten along with," he agreed.

Laurel nodded, and then there was a long pause as her mind bounced topics.

"Do you really think what happened earlier at the festival was random?" She was having a difficult time buying into it. Her background could be coming into play, tainting her viewpoint and making her less objective, so she truly wanted to hear his opinion.

"I'm not ruling it out yet," he said. "Since it was the festival, there were plenty of new faces. I'd like to talk to some of the local businesses to see if they've seen anyone hanging around. If the incident was tied to your past, the perp would most likely have come to town for a few days first. He could have been watching you and checking out your schedule to see when a good time to strike might be."

"These people aren't likely to come straight at me," she pointed out. "They would make it look like an accident so there would be no investigation linking my death back to what happened in Chicago."

"Moving might have played into their hands. No one knows you around here," he pointed out. "And no one knows who they are either. It would make moving through town during a festival very easy."

"True. Hiding and staying under the radar does keep everyone at arm's length from my personal life." She'd been purposeful about hiding her real identity. There were advantages and disadvantages to both sides. His point was well made. Since no one really knew her, they wouldn't know to look out for out-of-towners. But if folks did know her, James or Ricky would have already been here. Would they have slipped in her cabin in the middle of the night? Would she have even heard them coming?

Icy fingers gripped her spine.

The saying, *caught between a rock and a hard place,* applied to this situation.

"My only answer is to keep moving then," she said.

"At some point, they'll tire and give up. It's not logical for James or Ricky to hold onto this grudge for years. All I have to do is outlast them. Stay one step ahead until I'm old news."

Griff lowered his head.

"What kind of life is that for you?" he asked. "And what if that 'one step ahead' advantage disappears and they catch up to you? Who will have your back? Who will step in if you can't? Who will you talk to when you can't take another day alone?"

Every single word coming out of his mouth scored a direct hit in the center of her chest.

"I don't want to be alone any longer," she admitted. "And yet the thought of putting anyone else in danger seems selfish."

"Not if the person is trained to deal with dangerous situations," he stated. "Give me time to investigate. Let me help you come up with a plan for your next move. I'll let you sleep in my jail if it makes you more comfortable until these jerks can be arrested for harassment. I'm good at my job. Let me show you."

She wanted to believe every one of his words along with the promises being made. Could he deliver? There was no question about his desire to. She'd heard good things about him as sheriff. Could his skills stand up to what she faced?

The thought of tucking her tail between her legs and leaving again didn't sit well. Plus, Griff had offered to let her stay in his jail if she needed to, in order to feel safe again. The wild part was that being *with him* gave her such a sense of calm in the storm surrounding her.

"I hear what you're saying and, believe me, it sounds

good. Too good, actually," she hedged. "It can't be real. It can't be this easy. And I can't allow myself to be a burden to this sweet town that has welcomed me with open arms, let alone the sheriff I feel like I could really fall for."

Had she really just said those words? The red blush crawled up her neck again, centering on her cheeks. She felt them burn and wished she could take those words back. They were out there now.

"I feel the same," he said, bringing his hand to hers, before linking their fingers. A sense of calm washed over her at his move, but could she afford to let herself get caught up in it?

"You make me want to have a normal life again, Griff. I'm not saying this is the be-all, end-all in my life, but being around you makes me want to go to festivals and try to get to know people in town. I want to make plans for the future," she said, withdrawing her hand before she could get too comfortable. They'd barely even kissed, and he was fast becoming the best thing that had ever happened to her.

Which engaged all her warning systems.

"Then stay. Let's figure out what is happening between us because I can assure you that I've never felt this way about anyone else," he said.

"It's dangerous," she countered.

"Yes. But don't you want to know how it turns out? Because if we're right and this feeling is what I think it is, it's a game-changer," he pointed out.

The thought scared and excited her all at the same time.

Could they afford the distraction? And what if it

didn't work out? What if he woke up tomorrow and realized he'd made a huge mistake in committing to help her, let alone try to date during this time? Where would that leave her?

"Leaving anything unfinished between us seems like a waste and a shame," she said. "On the other hand, staying focused might mean the difference between life and death."

"Sticking around and letting me help you whether we decide to do anything about our chemistry or not might mean the difference between life and death. I hate the thought of letting you walk out that door, get in your car, and drive off. Not knowing if you needed me will haunt me for the rest of my life." His honesty caught her off guard. It probably shouldn't, though. He'd been nothing but honest and protective so far.

Could she trust him with her life?

CHAPTER TWELVE

"I'll respect your opinion no matter what you decide." Griff had said his piece. The rest was up to Laurel.

"To be honest, it's difficult to keep a clear head when I'm anywhere near you," she said, as more of that red blush settled on her cheeks.

Griff muttered a curse when his cell phone started buzzing. He'd successfully ignored it the first time a few seconds ago. The persistent buzz convinced him there was something important he needed to attend to.

"Would you mind if I took this?" he asked. The interruption came at a critical time in their conversation. This was the moment Laurel was about to decide whether or not to trust him, and here he was being called away by something on his phone.

"Go ahead," she said. He couldn't quite read her enough to decide if the interruption bothered her or not. It had to remind her that he had other responsibilities. Even if he took a couple of vacation days, he couldn't be certain his job wouldn't interfere. It was the nature of his work, and as long as he was in town, folks would reach out to him. Sherry, his secretary, could field some of the calls. She would be good about making sure the right ones got through. But he was kidding himself if he believed he could walk away from work completely. It would be the equivalent of walking around town with blinders on.

He stood up as the phone buzzed a third time, fished it from his pocket, and then checked the screen.

"It's my secretary," he said. "I better take this."

Rather than sequester in the bathroom, he moved to the kitchen window and searched the tree line for any signs the person from earlier had returned.

"Hi, Sherry. What's going on?" he asked.

"Sorry to bother you on your day off," she started.

"Don't worry about it," he confirmed. "You know I'm here whenever you need me."

"I heard about what happened earlier," she started before stopping to take in a breath. "What you do in your free time is no one's business."

"Agreed," was all he said.

"Knowing what happened at the festival to your... *friend*...I just thought you might like to hear about another curious incident that happened a little while ago," Sherry said.

"You bet I do," he said. "What is it? What happened?"

"I got a call from Diane at Restful Acres. You know Diane Moss, right?" she asked.

"I should. We went to high school together," he said, wondering what had happened at Laurel's employer.

"Diane called to report a suspicious male lurking

around the parking lot," Sherry stated. "When the groundskeeper, Eddie, decided to go over to the guy and confront him, the man hopped into his vehicle and took off without ever going inside the building. And here's the kicker. He had a temporary license plate."

"Well, now, that does sound suspicious," Griff said. "Tell Diane that I'm on my way over."

"On it," Sherry said.

"Did Eddie get a description of the vehicle in question?" he asked.

"It's a white sedan, four doors," Sherry said. "It was pretty generic. He didn't get the make or model. Said it could have been a Nissan or a Honda for all he knew. Said he was too far away to really get a sense of the vehicle since there were other cars and trucks parked in the lot blocking his view."

"I'm guessing that means he was too far away to get any type of description of the guy in question as well," Griff said.

"Yes, that's right. Eddie did say the guy was wearing a Stetson and sunglasses," she said.

That matched pretty much half the population in Gunner.

"What about short or tall?" Griff probed.

"Eddie couldn't get a sense of height. Said the guy was average height and build," she continued.

"Thank you for the heads up," Griff stated. "I'll head over to Restful Acres now and speak to Diane."

"Are you sure that's a good idea?" Sherry asked. "I can send one of the deputies instead."

"No. I need to do it, and I'm taking Laurel with me

if she'll agree," he said. "Considering what happened at the festival and now this...when did this occur?"

"Only just now. Diane called right away. Said she got a bad feeling after word got around about what happened at the festival," Sherry supplied.

"Good." Diligent citizens were the best line of defense against crime. The average person made a bigger difference than most realized in terms of prevention. It was the reason neighborhood watches were so successful in decreasing burglaries, etc. Not that they'd been needed in Gunner in the past.

Life had been quiet for the past year. He could only hope this didn't signal another crime wave—like that which had haunted his cousins a year ago—was headed this way.

"Will you tell Diane to stay inside until I get there?" he asked.

"Done," she said before he ended the call.

Griff turned toward Laurel, who sat at her kitchen table, radiating tension.

"A suspicious male was at Restful Acres," he said. "I'd like you to come with me to investigate."

"Let's go," she said after pushing up to standing. "I want to do one thing before we leave though. Is that okay?"

"Go for it," he said.

She walked right over to him, pushed up on her tiptoes, and kissed him.

Her hands came up to his shoulders as he deepened the kiss. Her fingers dug into his skin as he looped his arms around her waist. Desire welled inside him with the force of a tsunami as their bodies collided in each other's arms.

Griff had never experienced such an overwhelming force of nature and he could only imagine how much more incredible sex with Laurel would be. If there was time and she wanted it too, he wouldn't hesitate to make love to her right there in the kitchen. The thought of heading out to Restful Acres before a lead dried up was the equivalent of a bucket of ice water poured over his head.

He pulled back first and then rested his forehead against hers while he tried to catch his breath.

"You're beautiful," he said to her. "I don't know if anyone has told you that lately."

"Don't say it," she said.

"Why not? It's the truth," he commented, curious as to why she didn't want to hear the compliment.

"Because it will only make me want to stay," she said.

"Then, I'm definitely saying it again until you either get sick of hearing it or start believing it. Because you are an incredible person and you should be complimented every day," he said. He had a strong sense that she hadn't kissed another man since the incident a couple of years ago. He considered the fact she had chosen him to be her first foray back an honor.

Griff let his hands linger on her lower back. He stood there for just a few seconds longer, not yet ready to break the trance that was Laurel. She smelled like dark roast coffee and fresh flowers. It reminded him of sitting outside on the back porch with a fresh cup after a spring shower when the landscape began to wake after winter's sleep. She was the breath of fresh air that had been missing his whole life and he intended to tell her at some point. She deserved to know someone felt that way about her before she took off and left Gunner in the rearview.

This wasn't the right time though.

"Ready?" he finally asked.

"Okay," she said before pulling back on a sigh. He couldn't help but wonder if that would be the last time he got to hold her in his arms. Had she just said goodbye?

———

Laurel grabbed a crossbody bag-style purse, before tucking her phone and keys inside. She had a slim wallet that held her ID and enough cash to survive for a week if she needed to bolt at short notice.

Griff's cell phone buzzed and her heart dropped. It had taken Laurel a long time to get past the feeling that every noise could mean Ricky or James was right behind her. The heart-pounding, breath-stealing feeling was unwelcomed. The fact it had returned meant all the work she'd done up to this point was for nothing. She was back to square one.

Muttering a curse under her breath, she palmed her keys and waited for another landmine to explode.

Griff said a couple of 'I see' and 'uh-huhs' into the phone before ending the call. He turned to her and said, "One of my deputies stopped the white sedan on a routine traffic stop."

He started urging them both toward the front door as he spoke.

"The driver is being detained," he said as he made it to the door and started unlocking the deadbolt.

The thought of coming face-to-face with Ricky or James tied her stomach in knots. On the one hand, she'd wanted to stand in front of them and tell them off since they'd started harassing her. On the other, it was hard to think about looking into those hard eyes again. Eyes that had been hardened by hate and years of anger.

Neither of them was a good person and they both deserved to go to jail for what they'd done to her. She also realized if a cop didn't mind harassing her, he'd probably crossed the line in other areas of his professional life too. He could be on the take or siding with criminals when it suited him, perhaps even framing innocent people to take the fall for someone else's crime. She suspected maybe a little of both.

Laurel followed Griff out to his personal vehicle, ever aware of the fact someone had been watching her from the trees. The thought sickened her stomach. Griff was clearly in his element. His expression was serious, and she'd noticed that he kept his large frame in between her and the tree line as they walked to his vehicle. He walked her to her door, shut it behind her, effectively closing her off from the outside. She breathed a little easier knowing she wasn't out in the open while walking to his vehicle. Thoughts could be strange.

In a few minutes, she might be coming face to face with her harasser. Was it Ricky? James? It had to be James. She would recognize him anywhere and with any disguise. He had light brown hair, tanned skin, and an inch-long scar above his left eyebrow. He'd said it came from playing hockey in his youth. She highly doubted it now that she'd seen another side to him. A side that would track her down after she'd left Chicago.

Griff claimed the driver's seat and within a few seconds, they were heading down the lane and toward Restful Acres. Work was a half hour drive from the cabin.

"Where are we headed exactly?" she asked.

"The driver was on his way toward town," Griff supplied. "My deputy caught him blowing through a stop sign five miles away from Restful Acres."

"I'm guessing there aren't a whole lot of vehicles with temporary tags on them," Laurel said. "Any idea who was driving?"

"The ID says Paul David," he supplied.

"What about a picture? Would one of your deputies be able to send a photo over?" she asked.

"He's being detained right now but I don't want to alert him of the fact we're suspicious of him for more than a traffic violation," Griff stated. "If we take a picture, and he's your guy, he might clue into the fact you're here."

"Makes sense," she agreed.

"Right now, he just thinks we're annoying small-town law enforcement," Griff said with a smirk.

"I'm guessing you've been underestimated before," she noted.

"That's right," he said. "Sometimes leaning into my Texas accent gives out-of-towners the impression we aren't too bright around here."

"Sounds like a solid strategy to get someone talking," she said.

"Like I said before, I grew up around law enforcement and have pretty much seen or heard just about everything imaginable," he said.

"Thank you," Laurel said.

His face scrunched up in confusion.

"For being one of the good guys," she clarified.

"When I give my word to someone, I stand on it," he said with the kind of conviction that made her believe every word.

A few minutes later, Griff pulled up behind his deputy's SUV.

"I'll be sure to get the driver to come out and into your view," Griff said. "You don't have to leave this vehicle. Also, you should know the windshield and all of the glass is bulletproof in this vehicle."

"Okay," she said, digesting the news. She took in a couple of breaths to steel her resolves.

Griff started out the driver's side. He stopped himself in the middle of opening the door. He leaned across the seat and kissed her. The kiss was sweet and tender, offering a reassurance she didn't realize she needed.

"Thank you," she said the minute their lips pulled apart.

"The next time we kiss, I don't want to have to look at my watch," he said.

A whole lot of anxiety and tension welled up inside her squeezing her chest as she watched him walk away. She did her best to breathe through it as the man in question took a couple of steps into the oncoming road. Laurel exhaled and shook her head.

The man might have only been standing there for a

few seconds, but he wasn't the right height or build to be James or Ricky.

Griff jogged back over to the driver's side and then popped his head inside the door.

"It's not him," she said. The sun was going down and exhaustion was finally taking its toll. All Laurel wanted to do was go home and hit the bed.

Griff shot her a knowing look, as though he could sense her disappointment. Not only was the nightmare not over but with the incident at the festival today, it was likely starting all over again.

CHAPTER THIRTEEN

"I was just checking out the place for my mother," the Stetson-wearing man said.

Griff leaned against his deputy's SUV, legs crossed at the ankles and arms folded. He'd seen the flash of disappointment in Laurel's eyes when he asked her if this was the guy.

They would keep at it until they found James or Ricky if she gave him the chance.

He fished his cell out of his front pocket and alerted his deputy that he was leaving. He instructed his deputy to call if anything else came up. His deputy had his phone in his hand. He glanced at the screen and then gave a brief nod before going back to his interview.

Then, Griff joined Laurel in the truck as she bit back a yawn.

"Are you ready to go back to the cabin?" he asked.

"I know the answer should be yes. However, I'm afraid to be alone there," she admitted.

"I had no plans to leave you alone. I can sleep in the

truck or on your couch. Personally, I can do either and have done both when needed," he said.

"There's no way I can let you sleep in your vehicle. You're definitely too long to fit on the couch. You can take the bed," she said with a whole mess of determination in her voice.

"Bed it is." Griff might have said that, but he had no intention of kicking her out of her own bed.

"I think I could sleep for two days," Laurel said. He could hear the weariness in her voice. Not to mention the fact she'd been awake for almost two days straight and should probably already be passed out next to him.

"I'll have Sherry call Diane to let her know we aren't coming. Lean the chair back and close your eyes if you want. I got sleep last night, so I'm okay," he said.

Laurel did.

By the time they made it back to the cabin, she was softly snoring, and it was probably the most endearing thing he'd ever heard. He located her keys inside her small handbag before carrying her inside and putting her to bed. She didn't so much as move when he gently set her down before removing her shoes. He pulled the covers over her and then returned to the living room to lock the doors.

First, he headed outside to his truck to grab his overnight bag. He always had one with him in case he needed to stay out all night, which happened from time to time on cases.

Griff dug around in the floorboard of the backseat until he found was he was looking for. He shouldered his backpack before heading back inside the cabin. Inside the backpack, he had a fresh pair of clothes, boxers and a clean t-shirt, and an overnight bag filled with toiletries. It was the little comforts that helped while he was on the road.

He looked out across the lake. It was one of those clear Texas nights where the sky seemed to go on forever. Stars dotted the velvet blue canopy as it stretched across the sky. This was his Texas. This was the place he loved.

As he approached the front door, and toed his boots off, he heard a noise inside. The shower turned on. Did he wake Laurel? She was probably just grabbing a quick shower and changing into sleeping clothes. Rather than disturb her, he used the kitchen sink to brush his teeth and wash his face.

While the water ran in the next room, he settled onto the couch, figuring he could catch a catnap while Laurel was in the shower. He closed his eyes and leaned his head back. He must have dozed off for a few minutes because the next thing he heard was the bedroom door closing.

Griff checked his watch and, sure enough, he'd conked out for a solid twenty minutes. Since the shower was free, he grabbed his cotton t-shirt along with boxers, and brought his toiletry kit into the bathroom.

He turned on the spigot then set up his things on the counter before shedding his jeans. His shirt, socks, and underwear topped the pile in that order.

The warm shower water helped him think after a long day. His mind snapped to the person in the woods. Could Tad have an unhealthy fixation on her? Or had James or Ricky come for her like they'd threatened?

Laurel had given him a whole lot to think about

today. He needed to digest the information and come up with an offensive plan. So far, he felt like all he'd done was play defense. First things first, he would ask Rustler for the report on the festival incident. In fact, one was most likely in his inbox already. He'd neglected his email today. Granted, it was supposed to be his day off.

He always checked his email.

There was something about the thought of unplugging completely from his life that sent his stress levels soaring. Staying in the know helped him stay on top of what was happening in his county.

A loud bang, like someone slamming against the wall caused the room to shake. Griff hopped out of the shower as fast as he could, worried Laurel had tripped over in the dark. She was so tired earlier that she might even be sleepwalking.

He barely toweled off let alone have time to cut the water off. He blotted his body just enough to keep his boxers from absorbing all the water. He grabbed his cotton t-shirt as he bolted out of the bathroom.

Flipping on the light might scare the bejesus out of Laurel, so he opened the door and let the light from the hallway be enough. Stepping inside the dark room, he couldn't see a thing yet.

And then a blow to his face struck and he felt his own blood squirt from his busted lip. An inch over and the punch would have landed on the bridge of his nose.

He flipped the light switch on as he reached for the gun that was usually in his holster out of instinct. Except he wasn't wearing one. His weapon was in the next room and of no use to him there. Whoever was in the room had ducked out of sight after throwing the punch.

And then he saw something that made his pulse jackhammer his ribs.

Laurel was on her side, lifeless, with a noose around her neck. He immediately scanned the area. His gaze locked onto a syringe on the nightstand. There was a vial, too, right beside the needle. Since running toward an injured person in an unsecured area was a rookie mistake, Griff threw his back against the wall instead and searched for the other person in the room.

Methodically, he moved inside until he caught a glimpse of feet on the other side of the dresser. For a split-second, he considered bolting into the living room in order to retrieve his weapon, but then the perp bounded from around the dresser with a wrench of some kind. He swung it at Griff, who ducked in the nick of time to miss the metal connecting with his face again. This must have been the weapon the perp had used to split Griff's lip.

In an instant, Griff recognized the perp from the descriptions Laurel had given him. It was James.

"You're in serious trouble, James," Griff said, purposely using the man's name. Doing so might surprise James and give Griff a second or two of a head start on throwing a punch or ducking from one.

In the next second, a knee came up. Griff hopped back. Thankfully, the knee fell short. But Griff was done playing defense.

"I'm an officer of the law," he said, needing to identify himself to the perp. "Put your hands where I can see them."

James sneered at Griff. This guy clearly didn't care.

"I said get your hands up," Griff demanded, using the commanding voice he reserved for such situations. The next punch Griff caught with his bare hand. He squeezed, watching James' face scrunch up in pain. With Griff's free hand, he made a play for the wrench. Missed.

The darn thing came at him, landing hard against his chest. At least it wasn't his face this time. He let out a grunt and then went for the tackle. Griff had a definite size advantage over James. The pair flew into the nightstand, but James took the brunt of the hit.

A string of swear words followed a groan from James, who immediately went ballistic. Kicking, punching, and shouting, the man landed a few lucky hits but not enough to do any real damage. He had nothing to lose, considering he'd already assaulted an officer. Not good.

Griff had the momentary advantage of being on top. He used it to dig his knees into James' side and then twist the guy around as much as possible so he'd be face down on the carpet. Somewhere in the scuffle, the wrench disappeared.

A blood-curdling scream startled Griff. It took a second to realize Laurel was standing behind him. James made an attempt to kick her, but Griff grabbed the man's leg in time to stop him from making contact.

And then the wrench appeared in Laurel's hands. James fought hard against Griff, trying to get to her.

"No more," she said before whacking James across the face with the heavy metal instrument.

His head snapped to the right before his gaze

unfocused.

"Ohmygod. Did I kill him?" Laurel asked, dropping the wrench before slinking down on the bed. She was clearly in shock, but he was relieved the contents of the vial had clearly never made it into her body.

"Are you okay?" he asked, then qualified it by saying, "Physically?"

"I believe so," she said. "The last thing I remember is a pillow being shoved over my face."

She seemed to realize there was a noose around her neck in that moment as her hands came up to feel her face and neck. She gasped.

"Hold on a minute," he said. "I need to secure this guy. He is breathing and will regain consciousness at some point in the near future, if I had to guess. Can you grab zip cuffs from my backpack and bring them here?"

"Yes," Laurel said before disappearing down the hall. She returned a minute later and held out her hand. It was obvious that she was in shock but was still able to follow directions.

Griff turned James onto his stomach before zip cuffing his hands behind his back. Griff searched the man for a weapon and found a knife with a serious blade. He removed it and placed it out of the perp's reach.

"Can you call 911?" he asked Laurel. "Tell them you're with me at the yellow cabin and we need assistance."

"Yes," she said. Her movements were mechanical but she was coherent and able to follow orders.

After she ended the call, she returned to the bed and sat looking dumbfounded.

"You're okay," Griff reassured. "We got him and he can no longer hurt you."

"Yeah?" she asked but it was more statement than question.

"That's right. It's over," he said as the first tears spilled down her cheeks. It took all of Griff's self-discipline not to reach out to her, hold her. Be her comfort. But he had no plans to move until James was headed into custody and toward the back of a service vehicle.

"I'm sorry, I don't mean to cry," she said, wiping her cheeks.

"Don't be. Crying after we were born was how the doctors knew we were alive," he said, hoping the anecdote offered some reassurance.

Laurel gave a small smile through her tears—tears that looked a whole lot like relief.

Not fifteen minutes later, the cabin was filled with people. Deputy Rustler arrived first, followed by a pair of EMTs, and then Sherry. Deputy Hernandez was next to arrive while Rustler photographed the crime scene and collected evidence.

James blinked his eyes open as he was hauled to his feet. He shook his head like he could somehow shake off the reality he was going to jail.

"Who are you working with?" Griff asked, figuring it couldn't hurt. Some criminals could get chatty once they had cuffs on. They probably thought it would make law enforcement go easy on them but that was a prosecutors job, not Griff's.

"No one," James stated. "I acted alone for my man Timothy."

"Your man?" Griff stated with disgust. "Don't you

mean your man the rapist?"

"Nah, man," James said. "Timothy didn't have to..." His voice trailed off when he saw Laurel sitting on the bed giving him a death stare.

"This is right up Ricky's alley," she said to him, her voice steady as a rock.

"He bailed a long time ago. Said it wasn't worth it," James said. "But I made a pact with Timothy and there was no way I was going back on it."

"Ricky sounds smarter than I thought," Griff stated. "Because you're the one who is going to spend the rest of his life behind bars."

"She disobeyed her man. She had it coming and then said Timothy tried to rape her," James said by way of defense.

"He did," was all Laurel said.

"No way," James argued. "He wouldn't."

"Oh yeah? How well did you really know him?" she countered. "Did you know he used to call you Dimwitted James behind your back?"

The words struck more fiercely than a physical blow.

"He wouldn't..." But the seeds of doubt were sewn in James's eyes. Doubt had taken seed and it was obvious in his expression.

"He did," she responded.

James's mouth dropped open.

"We're done here," Laurel stated.

Hernandez gave a quick look toward Griff, who nodded.

James was going away for a very long time. Griff had every intention of ensuring it. Laurel was safe now.

CHAPTER FOURTEEN

It took two hours for statements to be given, EMTs to check out Laurel and then Griff, and the cabin to empty out. A stray cat sauntered inside as the last person left.

"Who is this guy?" Griff asked, bending down to scratch the cat behind the ears.

"That's Henry, but he doesn't normally let anyone get close to him," Laurel said, the lost look in her eyes was gone now, replaced by a tentative smile.

"How about some milk, Henry?" Griff asked as the cat rubbed against his pant leg. "Looks like I have a new friend."

"So it does. I have a can of tuna if he's hungry," she said with more than a hint of surprise in her voice as she walked over to the cabinet.

Griff fixed a small coffee cup of milk. He caught Laurel's gaze. "You must be exhausted by now."

She shook her head.

"I finally feel free," she said. "Really free."

"It's over," he agreed.

"I don't ever want to sleep again," she said before opening the can and placing a small amount of tuna on a plate. She bent down and set the plate next to the milk cup. "Which I know isn't realistic but I'm not tired in the least. Not right now."

She stood up and smiled as Henry went for the tuna.

Griff figured it was now or never. He needed to tell her how he felt before he found an excuse not to.

"I've waited a long time for someone like you to walk into my life," Griff said to her as they stood there in the kitchen with Henry at their feet. "I'm not a kid and I've dated a whole lot of people. Enough to know when someone special walks into my life." He reached out and took her hands in his. The current of electricity running through him was a comfort now.

The look in her eyes encouraged him to keep going.

His heart pounded wildly inside his chest because for the first time, if this person walked out of his life, he realized he would feel the ripples of that decision for the rest of his life. So, he dropped down on one knee.

"You deserve to know how I feel before you make the decision to stay or leave," he continued, staring into those beautiful blue eyes of hers. Now that the threat was gone, she was free to roam and he wondered if she would consider staying in Gunner.

Her expression was unreadable and despite facing stab wounds, bullets, and all manner of destructive forces, saying these next words was the scariest thing he'd ever done or would ever do. There was no denying the fact he'd fallen hard for the big-eyed beauty.

"I don't want to scare you with what I'm about to say, but I think you should know that I've fallen in love with you, Laurel. I'm in love with you." Saying anything more might just cause her to jump up, get in her car, and ditch him forever, so he waited to hear her response.

A slow, beautiful smile spread across her face.

"I knew from the second we met there was something very different about you, Griff Quinn," she started. "Believe me when I say that I never believed in love at first sight. Until you. Getting to know you has opened my eyes to what an incredible and caring human being you are. I love you and I count myself the luckiest person in the world that you feel the same way."

Griff shot up to his feet, pulling her into an embrace. He kissed her lips, her chin, her neck. He slowly skimmed his lips across her skin until he reached her mouth again. He claimed it with bruising need this time.

His pulse skyrocketed and his heart thundered in his chest.

He slowly made his way down the nape of her neck and back up until his mouth was within an inch of her ear, and then he whispered, "You should know that I'm all in when it comes to this relationship. And I mean that. You have my word. You have my heart. And when you're ready, if that day ever comes, you can have my forever. I'd like you to do me the great honor of marrying me."

Laurel's hands came up to frame Griff's face. She brushed the backs of the fingers on her right hand against his cheek when she caught his gaze.

"Griffin Quinn, I don't need a whole lot of time to know what we have is special. If you're asking me to marry you right now, my answer is yes," she said, and his heart danced.

"Yes?" Griff needed to hear confirmation just to be sure he could trust his own ears.

"My answer is yes," she said. "I will be your wife. I will marry you. And I will love you for the rest of my life."

"I have only one request," he said, mustering a serious expression.

"Oh yeah? What's that?" she asked.

"Two actually," he realized.

"Okay. What are your two requests?" she asked.

"One, we nab Mrs. Brubaker at least once a week for dinner at our place," he said with a smile.

"Done," she said. "I don't even have to think about that one. She would love that."

He smiled.

"And the second?" she asked.

"I've always wanted a pet. A cat actually. We have to adopt Henry and give him a home," he said as a smile spread across her face.

"That's a no-brainer," she said. "I'm happy to give this sweet kitty a permanent home."

"That's all I need to hear," he said before scooping his bride-to-be in his arms.

"But first, I need to make a call. There's someone I need to speak to," she said with a serious expression.

"Whatever you need to do." He set her down so she could grab her phone and then took a step back. "Do you need privacy?"

"No," she said as the corners of her lips upturned. "This will only take a few seconds."

She punched in a number and then put the cell to her ear.

"Marissa, it's me," she began as the smile widended. "How are you?" She said a few uh-huhs into the phone. "How are the babies?"

Now, the smile had spread across her beautiful face.

"Good. I want to hear all about them and how you guys are doing," she continued. "Can I call you tomorrow?" A brief pause was followed by, "I've missed you too. Everything is okay now. I'm not leaving your life again."

When she ended the call, she beamed.

"They're good," she said. "And we're going to have a 'coffee date' tomorrow via the phone to catch up on all that's been happening."

"That's good news," he said, picking her up again. She wrapped her arms around his neck and kissed him.

"Thank you," was all she said. "You're amazing."

"I can say the same thing about you," he said before carrying her into the next room and into bed. This cabin might be a temporary space, but there was no doubt in his mind that he'd found his permanent home in Laurel.

He kissed her, long and slow.

Home.

———

Griff's cell buzzed before the sun came up the next morning. He had half a mind to ignore it. Except it could be bad news.

"I'd better check to see what that is," he said to

Laurel. Her eyes glittered with desire and she'd never been more beautiful to him than right then.

"Okay," she said, pushing up to sitting on the bed.

He scrambled to locate his cell before the call rolled into voicemail. There it was, hiding underneath his backpack. He grabbed it and answered with surprise. What was his father doing calling?

"Griff here."

"Hey, son," Archer Quinn said.

"Sir," Griff stated. His father had always insisted on a formal greeting.

"Harding was shot," his father said.

"When? Where?" Griff asked as more questions pounded the backs of his eyelids.

"All I know is he was serving a warrant when it happened and he's in surgery now," his father said.

Griff's heart dropped.

"When will he be home?" he asked.

"I'm headed to the hospital now," his father said. "Austin General. Get there as soon as possible."

With that, the call ended.

"Is everything okay?" Laurel asked a stunned Griff.

"It's one of my brothers. He was shot on the job," Griff stated as the shock and horror of that statement started to sink in.

"I'm so sorry," Laurel said. Her forehead creased with concern and she immediately jumped into action. "Is he okay?"

"We'll know by the time we get there," he said. At least, he hoped there would be good news.

"What can I do?" she asked.

"Go to the hospital with me?" he asked.

"I'll throw on clothes and be ready in five," she said.

He needed to do the same. And then he needed to get on the road. He might not have spoken to his brother in the past ten years, but Quinns would always be there for each other when the chips were down. This was no exception. Even if the last time they spoke had been one helluva argument.

"Would it be okay if I call Marissa on the way?" she asked. "I don't want to disappear on her again."

"Of course. I want you to have everything your heart desires," he stated and meant every word as he kissed his bride-to-be.

And then prayed his brother would survive.

CHAPTER FIFTEEN

Epilogue

Of all the bad days in life, and Harding had had plenty, he could not believe he'd been shot. As a U.S. Marshal, he'd been well trained to perform his duties. Granted, it was his job to put away men who had nothing to lose. That was never good. But he was the best at his job. So why him? How had this happened to him?

Blinking through blurry eyes, he listened to the *beep, beep, beep* of the machine next to his bed in the hospital. Harding had a good mind to rip the IV out of his arm and go get the S.O.B. who'd fired a wild shot and scored a direct hit.

He wanted details as to how he could have gotten so sloppy but couldn't seem to come up with any. It was the medication he was on. Harding wasn't a fan of pain killers. He planned to refuse the next round when the nurse came by. Considering the fact he had to fight to stay conscious, he must be on too many.

All they did was dull his thinking.

Could he sit up? The effort didn't produce much. He barely moved. He couldn't force his eyes to open, and his arms felt like literal lead weights. Frustration ripped through him. For someone who didn't sit down for more than two minutes unless he was behind the wheel, his present circumstance was infuriating.

Maybe he could call for the nurse. Nope. It was like his mouth was in cahoots with his eyes and arms. Nothing worked the way it was supposed to.

An ominous feeling settled over Harding as a question formed in the back of his mind, vying for attention. He struggled to push the question to the forefront of his thoughts. He needed to know what his brain was trying to ask.

After a few minutes of effort, it finally pushed through. He couldn't move his arms or legs. Were painkillers responsible? Or was this going to be something permanent?

Harding railed against the idea. He would have remembered something so drastic as being paralyzed, wouldn't he? Then again, his brain was wired to protect him. Would it hide something so important? Bury it deep?

Refusing to accept the possibility that he wouldn't be able to move in the same way as before, he made a fist with his left hand.

Thankfully, it worked. Could he capitalize? He forced his arm to move next. Then, his right leg. Small movements were as far as he could get. He hoped this was the beginning and not the end of what he would be able to do.

. . .

Click here to read Harding's story.

ALSO BY BARB HAN

Don't Mess With Texas Cowboys

Texas Cowboy's Protection

Texas Cowboy Justice

Texas Cowboy's Honor

Texas Cowboy Daddy

Texas Cowboy's Baby

Texas Cowboy's Bride

Texas Cowboy's Family

Texas Cowboy Sheriff

Texas Cowboy Marshal

Cowboys of Cattle Cove

Cowboy Reckoning

Cowboy Cover-up

Cowboy Retribution

Cowboy Judgment

Cowboy Conspiracy

Cowboy Rescue

Cowboy Target

Crisis: Cattle Barge

Sudden Setup

Endangered Heiress

Texas Grit

Kidnapped at Christmas

Murder and Mistletoe

Bulletproof Christmas

For more of Barb's books, visit www.BarbHan.com.

ABOUT THE AUTHOR

Barb Han is a USA TODAY and Publisher's Weekly Bestselling Author. Reviewers have called her books "heartfelt" and "exciting."

Barb lives in Texas--her true north--with her adventurous family, a poodle mix and a spunky rescue who is often referred to as a hot mess. She is the proud owner of too many books (if there is such a thing). When not writing, she can be found exploring Manhattan, on a mountain either hiking or skiing depending on the season, or swimming in her own backyard.

Made in the USA
Coppell, TX
10 March 2022

74774938R00113